AFT

'Martine McDonagh wri[...]
and unsentimentally a[...]
Stephen May, Costa Prize-shortlisted author of
Life! Death! Prizes!
and *Wake Up Happy Every Day*

'A great read.'
Araminta Hall, author of
Everything and Nothing,
and *Dot*

'After Phoenix is a raw, emotive portrayal of a family
pushed to its limits by grief.'
Lizzie Enfield, author of
What You Don't Know, and
Uncoupled

'Given that the book's subject is grief, and that grief is a
dulling, leaden, grey and tedious feeling, it's amazing how
vital, entertaining and even funny *After Phoenix* is,
without in any way shortchanging the reality
of the experience.'
Caustic Cover Critic

'In this moving portrait of not only what comes after loss
but what comes after that, McDonagh demonstrates more
finesse on the subject than anyone in recent memory.'
Caught In The Carousel

ABOUT THE AUTHOR

After Phoenix is Martine McDonagh's second novel.
Her first novel, *I Have Waited, and You Have Come*, was published in
2006 and 2012. *After Phoenix* was written with support from the
Arts Council England's Grants for the Arts scheme.
Martine McDonagh has published short fiction in *Quick Fictions*,
The Illustrated Brighton Moment and *The Brighton Book* and is an
occasional contributor to *Writing* magazine. She has a Creative Writing MA from Manchester Metropolitan University and works as an
artist manager and lecturer in the music industry.

AFTER PHOENIX

MARTINE McDONAGH

Published by Ten to Ten Publishing, 2013, 2014

ISBN: 978-0-9575037-3-1

Copyright © Martine McDonagh, 2014

A CIP catalogue record for this book is available from the
British Library.

www.martinemcdonagh.com

This book is dedicated to
Carol McDonagh

Phoenix
(Merry Xmas Everybody)

O N ACCOUNT OF HIS MOTHER KATHERINE'S resistance to him having a motor bike for Christmas, Phoenix had chosen not to reveal that his only previous attempt at riding one - not a motor bike per se but his friend Tim's moped - had resulted in him losing control and driving through Tim's neighbour's privet and onto their front lawn. It had cost him fifty quid from his savings to straighten out the front forks and replace the visor on Tim's helmet, never mind the weeks of suffering as his friends mimed collisions with walls, doors and teachers in school corridors, pubs and shops. As it turned out, Phoenix wasn't the only one with a secret motorcycling past, although his father JJ's was less embarrassing.

They were in the showroom when JJ announced to the salesman that he had once owned a Norton Commando. He'd sold it when Katherine fell pregnant with Phoenix and used the money to purchase a 1954 baby blue Ford Consul with full width red leather seats; a greater compromise than intended, he explained to the salesman, what with Henry Ford being a fascist and all that, but it had to be said it was a beautiful machine with a wonderfully symmetrical registration number: YOY 414.

That story there, Phoenix told himself, and the fact of that being the first time he had heard any of it, offered a perfect illustration as to why he and his father weren't closer. JJ, self-appointed man of the people, preferred talking to - or at least at - strangers. He would dig up some common ground regardless of whether or not they were in agreement on the important thing - the important thing being politics - and relate in passing to them the facts about his life he so casually omitted to share with his first born child and only son.

Weaving in and out of the rows of bikes on display, Phoenix spotted his from the back first: PJJ 238. Phoenix John Jacobs. 238. If only he'd been born on the twenty-third of August. It was the colour of the foil wrapping on Christmas chocolate money. Not gold, that would be limp as hell. Metallic yellow. 'Oi Dad, come and see.'

Later that evening, JJ was at the sink, locked on to Katherine's back as she washed up. With his arms around her waist and his chin resting on her shoulders, he wittered on, something about Japanese motor companies killing off British industry by producing high-quality machines with low running costs.

'I'll take that as a thumbs up for the bike then,' said Phoenix and kissed his mother on the cheek where his dad wasn't. As an afterthought, he patted his father on the shoulder. 'Thanks Mum, thanks Dad. I promise not to go mad on it,' he said, and sloped off to find Penny, who was stretched out on the sofa watching *Crossroads* with Wedgie the cat perched on her uppermost hip and Benn curled up against her belly.

'Seen me boik?' Phoenix did his best Benny from *Crossroads* impersonation.

'Yeah, smart,' she said without looking at him.

'See the numberplate?'

'Fan. Dabby. Dozy,' said Penny.

'What's the matter with you? You should be kissing my feet, you'll get a much better Christmas present now thanks to me and my bike.' No response. 'I can't believe you still watch this moronic tosh.'

'It's good.'

'No it isn't. You're in love with Sandy.' He raised his voice to a squeak. 'Oh Penny, forget about David Cassidy, he's not a real man. Run away with meeeeee.'

'For god's sake, bugger off.' Penny pulled a cushion from the pile behind her head and threw it at him. The cats scarpered, the opening shots of a major battle only too familiar to them. Phoenix picked up the jettisoned cushion and Frankenstein-walked it towards the settee. Penny screamed: 'Daaaaad!'

Early on Christmas morning, the roads were clear of traffic and the weather conditions mild and dry and ideal for a maiden solo voyage, so Phoenix prepared to set off for the first time without his father. In the sitting room, one of the cats was under the Christmas tree tearing the wrapping paper off a present with its teeth. Katherine and Penny were both still asleep. JJ was already up and working in the Doghouse, as he did every Christmas morning to demonstrate that the consumerist or religious (depending on his mood) festival held no meaning for him. A stance he would maintain until it was time for him to open his presents.

Phoenix had grown so fast as a child, it had been normal for him to be bought clothes a size too big: trousers, shoes, coats. There was always an solution to this problem: turned-up cuffs, socks doubled over at the toe. It was nothing out of the ordinary that his new crash helmet wobbled a bit, as if it were balancing on the topmost point of his skull. He didn't mention it to JJ, partly because he didn't want to appear ungrateful, but mainly because he didn't want to have to stop riding his bike until the helmet could be swapped for one the right size. Instead he solved the problem by piling his long hair up on top of his head and clamping his helmet down onto it to keep it steady.

***

ON BOXING DAY EVENING Phoenix was bored. He'd been out on his own, but he hadn't yet plucked up the courage to ride his bike in the dark. Katherine and JJ were out at the Christmas do for Gingerbread, the charity where Katherine volunteered, helping single mothers and their ungrateful brats. His default entertainment was to lie on his bed and think about sex, his bike and sex on his bike. But even this was being hindered by the stop-start racket from Penny's bedroom. She was apparently incapable of listening to a record - even a single - all the way through from start to finish, so enamoured was she of the process of lifting one record over the spindle and balancing the next one in its place on her new music centre. If not that, she was bashing down, seemingly with her fist, on the stop, rewind and play buttons of its cassette deck.

He decided to brave the dark and ride down to the village to Rob's house. It was less than a mile away and there was no traffic, but it wasn't only the dark that was putting him off. When Rob, supposedly his best and definitely his oldest friend, had come round before Christmas he'd shown no interest in Phoenix's first term at university and behaved as if he hadn't been away at all. The banter was the same, the in-jokes, the nicknames, but they'd become weightless in the absence of shared experience.

Parking his bike on the drive at Rob's parents' house, he half-expected his friend to come to the door like in the old days. When he didn't, he let himself in to find Rob there alone with a tea tray at his feet, strewn with cigarette papers, stray strands of tobacco and the shreds of a Christmas card. The TV was so loud Phoenix wondered if Rob had turned it up in the hope it might make more sense to his addled brain, or if his deaf granny had been for a Christmas visit and nobody had thought to lower the volume after she'd gone. It was only when Phoenix lowered the volume that Rob acknowledged his presence.

''Right you old bastard?' he said, without averting his eyes from the screen, where Bambi was slithering, legs akimbo, over an icy pond. *Disney Time with Paul and Linda McCartney* was more interesting than a visit from his best friend.

Rob waved his joint towards Phoenix, and when Phoenix shook his head withdrew the offer with the same level of disinterest. They sat in silence until the end of the Bambi clip. And Phoenix was never more aware of his own limbo state, suspended as he was between two lives and integrated into neither. He consoled himself with the notion that solitude was the lot of the Chosen.

'I'm dying,' said Rob, his eyes squinted in the plume of smoke that curled from his nostrils as he spoke.

'*What*?'

Rob collapsed forward over his knees in uncontrollable but somehow still uninfectious cackles.

'Fuckinell you bastard, I thought you were serious,' said Phoenix.

Never mind that they were drifting apart existentially,

they appeared to be in separate physical locations: Rob was in a room full of people, noisy, laughing, snogging, drinking, dancing, sharing a smoke, while Phoenix was sitting in the corner of a wood-chipped room, watching, his shirt buttoned up to the neck, ignored up close but whispered about at a distance.

Jesus, Rob's smoking was making him, Phoenix, paranoid!

'You still coming on New Year's Eve?' said Phoenix.

''Course,' said Rob, heaving himself up in his chair like an old man. 'Wouldn't miss it for the you-know-what.'

Another cartoon started, Snow White and the Seven Dwarves, and Rob sang along quietly to himself: '*Hi ho, hi ho, It's off to work we go.*'

'Right then,' said Phoenix. 'Time I was off too.'

'Right then,' said Rob. He clearly had no idea if Phoenix had been there ten minutes or ten days, but took his departure as a signal to lift the tea tray on to his knees and roll another joint.

'I'll give you a ring to remind you about the party,' said Phoenix from the door.

He'd been out for less than an hour and wasn't ready to go home. He decided to drive down to his old primary school for a look at the playground where, at the age of nine, he had failed his cycling proficiency test by steering his pushbike over the foot of the examiner.

The school was at the end of a long twisting cul-de-sac on an estate of newish, boxy houses with thin brick walls and large windows. Penny's best friend, Jackie, lived in one of them, but he wasn't sure which. He was sure though that she fancied him; she'd been at their house every evening since he came home. He imagined her spying on him from behind net curtains tinted orange and green by Christmas lights, but in all likelihood she was over at his house again, snogging his sister.

He drew up at the school gates and directed his headlamp's beam into the playground. Look at how the boy's come on, he wanted to shout, but didn't, he was already worried that the rumble of the bike's engine was disturbing the quiet street. He turned the bike with difficulty in the narrow road, not yet used to the weight of it, then pulled back on the throttle to rev the engine, taking off with such a jerk he had to clench his groin to keep from falling off during what was to become, in the retelling, his first wheelie. Heart pounding, he rounded the corner at speed then slowed the bike right down and steered it towards home.

JJ's Citroen DS was crouched, apparently without wheels, in the darkness. And it might as well have been up on bricks for all the use it got. Phoenix reckoned it hadn't moved since they had driven him to Oxford in September. Its last outing before that would have been to France for the family summer holiday.

While any other family of modest means in Great Britain was discovering Spain, returning home with wicker donkeys and hand-painted castanets for their windowsills and mantlepieces, the Jacobs family had never once pointed the bonnet of the DS over the Franco-Iberian border. JJ's justification for staying on the French side of the Pyrenees was that if they wanted 'that kind of holiday', he could drive them home and drop them off at Butlin's. Accusations of snobbery from Katherine forced him into the somewhat loftier argument that tourism was the new imperialism. Discuss. This was the kind of forgettable argument that was guaranteed to keep his parents entertained and Penny's hands clamped over her ears all the way from Calais until the views from the Peripherique diverted their attention towards the distant landmarks of Paris.

Indoors, T-Rex was blasting from the speakers of Penny's music centre, and judging by the rhythmic thudding on the living room ceiling, she and Jackie were either rehearsing a clog dance or were in the throes of lesbian sex. If only he'd had the foresight to drill a peephole in the ceiling. The way Penny copied her friend was hilarious: same hairstyle, same clothes, eyebrows tweezed into the same high arch. She even exaggerated her Bristol accent to sound more like Jackie, and she probably only bought *Jackie* comic every week because it had the little tart's name on the front. Lezzer.

He plundered a bottle of Guinness from the sideboard, switched on the telly to distract his thoughts from the imagined goings-on upstairs, and sat down in the chair closest to the fire. He stretched out his long legs and took a swig of his beer. The girls would come to him soon enough - like ash to an ashtray - he could wait.

***

PHOENIX SAT AT THE KITCHEN TABLE, flicking through an old copy of the *Bristol Evening Post* without really reading it and wondering what it would be like to have a father who didn't cut windows out of every page of the paper before anyone else had the chance to read it.

The Jacobses had never been short of help from Phoenix's friends to get the house ready for their party on New Year's Eve, but Phoenix expected this year might be different given the lukewarm reception to his homecoming. So when Rob let himself in at the back door, shivering from his walk up from the village and with a banging hangover from another night spent in front of the television, Phoenix was taken by surprise.

Rob, apparently oblivious to Phoenix's presence even in his own home, set about helping himself to breakfast. He cut two thick slices of bread, cracked an egg into the pan on the Aga and made himself a sandwich of it and two cold sausages foraged from the fridge. Phoenix knew better than to interrupt Rob while he was eating, so continued to flick while his friend stood at the kitchen sink, scoffing his greasy sandwich and looking out over the garden, like an explorer might look back over newly-traversed wastes and contemplate the next stage of his journey. Only Rob was at his final stop. Unless he was planning to leave again as soon as he'd eaten without so much as a word to anyone. Stoner.

Rob stuffed the last mouthful into his gob, wiped his greasy palms on his donkey jacket and, despite Katherine and JJ's absence, said: 'Thanks, Mr. and Mrs. J. That was just the job.' He washed up his eggy pan and the cups and plates that had accumulated on the counter in the hours since dinner the night before, a chore Phoenix had never seen him undertake at home, but one he embraced so naturally at the Jacobs' house.

Phoenix and Rob still hadn't spoken when Katherine appeared in the kitchen, wrapped in JJ's dressing gown, her hair all tousled and magnificent. In the absence of a belt she clutched the front of the dressing gown with one hand, and with the other she blew a kiss to the boys. Rob was engrossed in constructing a roll-up, which to Phoenix's relief contained nothing more incriminating than tobacco, but stopped momentarily to look up and bellow, 'Morning Mrs. J.!'

Katherine opened the back door to call JJ in from the Doghouse: 'Breakfast!' Meaning, of course, that he was to come in and make hers - he would have eaten his own hours before. Penny, keen to put in her own breakfast order, appeared seconds later, also in her dressing gown. On a sudden whim, Phoenix checked the temperature of the air between his sister and Rob in case something had happened between them that might be making Rob awkward in Phoenix's company, but if Penny noticed Rob at all it was with the same level of fascination you might show a piece of old broken furniture you keep forgetting to throw out.

It was afternoon before the party preparations were properly underway. Phoenix and Rob were in charge of the sitting room; it was their job to push the large items of furniture against the walls to allow as much space as possible for dancing and to remove anything small or breakable (there was nothing of particular value because the Jacobses didn't value material possessions, nor were they sentimental) to other parts of the house. Penny's job was, as it had been for the previous six years, to mix the dough for cheese straws. As usual she complained that they could have bought ready-made from the supermarket in the village without anyone being able to tell the difference, and as usual Phoenix reminded her that she had two legs and the capability to walk to said supermarket and purchase said cheese straws if she felt that strongly about it.

Helpers came and went in dribs and drabs throughout the afternoon, delivering wine, beer, cider and home-made party food: vol-au-vents, sausages on sticks, pineapple and cheese on sticks, a trifle, more cheese straws and a chocolate cake that didn't stand a hope of still being there when the party kicked off. Some people stopped to help, others for a chat and a drink, happy to let their kids be thrown around the living room for a while by Phoenix and Rob, but most shouted their greetings over the noise, left their offerings in the kitchen and went home again to change into their party clothes.

At five o'clock Katherine summoned everyone into the sitting room for her ritual celebration of her daughter's birth (or at least the labour that preceded it). As usual Penny tried to sneak off to her room. And as usual Phoenix anticipated her attempt to escape and blocked the doorway.

'It's not even anything to do with me,' said Penny as Phoenix grabbed her arm. 'If she wants to celebrate hours of excruciating pain, that's up to her, but I don't see why we all have to suffer with her every bloody year.'

'Now now, young sprog,' said Phoenix. 'We've all had to suffer you for all these years, so let your mummy have her moment of remembering what life was like without you.'

Katherine extracted her battered copy of *La Traviata* from the pile next to the gramophone and showed the sleeve to them each in turn, like a magician preparing the audience for her next trick. She folded back the door of the gramophone, slipped the record over the spindle and proceeded to sing along at full volume, in Italian, a language she had no knowledge of beyond the few syllables she'd accumulated by repeating this same performance every New Year's Eve for the past fifteen years. She waved her arms like a conductor, encouraging the others to join in and everyone except Penny obliged, shouting out foreign half-words like irregular churchgoers battling with an unfamiliar hymn.

Phoenix sympathized with Penny to some degree as she squirmed under his grasp; it probably was unusual for a woman to wail her favourite arias during labour and it was probably more unusual to carry on the practice once the pain was over, to want to celebrate each contraction, but Phoenix enjoyed the occasion all the more for its abnormality.

All the things that embarrassed his sister about their parents, Phoenix loved. He adored that they would take off on impulse and drive for miles to see a play, especially one written by some nobody and performed by a gaggle of amateurs in a village hall in the middle of nowhere. He loved that Katherine would send JJ out to buy fish and chips rather than wash the dishes. They had passion, Katherine and JJ; they embraced life and all its unpredictability. Especially its unpredictability. They had no fear of being blown off course. They didn't care what people thought of them, and that's how he wanted to be.

Rob collapsed onto the sofa for a snooze and Phoenix wandered into the kitchen, where Katherine was rummaging in the cutlery drawer in search of the bottle opener that was already on the counter next to the bottles.

JJ was attempting to pin an envelope, containing two tickets (Phoenix's Christmas present to his parents) for the Carpenters concert at the Colston Hall, to the dresser without making a new hole. There were plenty of existing holes, drilled by long-dead woodworm, but they were all too big and the pin kept falling out. JJ gave up and jabbed it into the solid wood at the edge of an old hole.

'Okay Dad,' said Phoenix. 'Who's the most talented Carpenter?'

'No idea,' said JJ. 'Jesus? He made some nice furniture. If you're inclined to believe the stories.'

The pin dropped out again and Phoenix snatched up the fallen envelope from the dresser.

'Come on Dad,' he said, waving the envelope in his father's face. 'Richard or Karen. Ricky or Sticky. Say who's the best.'

JJ snatched the envelope back. 'Karen,' he said. Then, because it was an unwritten rule in the Jacobs household to always say why you thought what you thought, he added, 'Because if something ever happened to Richard, if he smashed up his hands in an accident, say, she could always carry on her career without him.'

'Hey Mum, what do you think?' Phoenix knew she wouldn't be able to resist.

'Ridiculous,' she said. 'Just because she *could* carry on, it doesn't mean she would, or should.'

Having set things off nicely, Phoenix stepped back to

15

observe, like an umpire watching a fast rally at Wimbledon. But his concentration kept slipping because he was also on the lookout for Jackie. He'd answered the phone earlier when she'd called to speak to Penny, and told her he'd be waiting for her, to which she'd responded by asking him if he was pissed already. He wasn't, of course, but he liked that she thought of him as a drinker, it made him feel wild and rugged, like Peter Fonda on his chopper in Easy Rider, his hair blown back by the breeze, as opposed to the namby-pamby dry-weather-rider in a helmet purring along at thirty miles per hour he was in reality.

Rob resurfaced, refreshed by his nap, and joined Phoenix at the kitchen table having ripped the tab from the top of their cornflakes box to use in the construction of a joint.

''Right there, our Peeniss?'

Through primary school Phoenix's friends had struggled to settle on a satisfactory abbreviation of Phoenix's name – their own names were easily shortened: Robin to Rob; Michael, Mike; Timothy, Tim and so on – but by their first year at secondary school they had all, even Phoenix, agreed on Pinhead. He was gangly, with wider hips and narrower shoulders than your average male, and his face was long and narrow, so even he had to admit that the name seemed to fit. When they hit sixth form though, just as Phoenix was priming himself to burst forth into the female community, or at least into the girls' corner of the common room, as a candidate for sexual partnership, Pinhead matured into Peeniss, a sobriquet delivered with so much hissing and suggestion of sexual prowess that, just as a plant will droop from over-watering, any idea of advancement in the shagging department wilted too. And so, it was no fault of his own that Phoenix was still a virgin.

He switched on the radio, turning it up loud to fill the silence that would once have been conversation between him and Rob. Fluff Freeman was counting down the Top Sixty for the year. Rob and Phoenix groaned simultaneously, as they would at the introduction of each of the next thirty-five songs, but they listened anyway, and when Rob offered Phoenix a toke on his spliff he gave in and accepted and the music got better and better, until at last they were drumming on the table and singing along in their best falsetto to Limmie and the Family Cooking.

Phoenix was slow to register the minor commotion that was Penny trying to smuggle Jackie in through the front door. The front hall was the one corner of the house where all noises converged, but even the clash of ongoing rhythms - a blue-lipped Violetta wheezing her way through the finale of *La Trav* in the sitting room; 'Welcome Home' by Peters and Lee and Rob at number nineteen in the kitchen; Gary Glitter chugging away in Penny's bedroom - struggled to overwhelm the girls' squealing reunion after a whole twenty-four hours apart.

Phoenix poked his head around the kitchen door to see Jackie hand Penny a large blue Tupperware container, its lid and walls misted with condensation from the warmth of its contents. Jackie's contribution to the party the year before had been a mountain of tiny pink-and-white iced cakes that her mother had helped her to make from a packet mixture. He remembered because Penny had challenged Phoenix and JJ to a blindfold taste-test to see if they could tell the difference between them and the home-made angel cake someone else had delivered; they'd both been too diplomatic to say the packet cakes had the taste and texture of cotton wool.

'I hope you're going to share those around,' he said, but they made a convincing pretence of not hearing him.

Phoenix clocked Jackie's hotpants and flesh-coloured tights and pondered whether or not she was wearing knickers. He watched her follow his sister up the stairs, trying to concentrate on the tiny bit of fabric that flared out where buttock met thigh, and sniggered at the thought of the two of them getting ready together, swapping clothes and smearing eyeshadow on each other, brown for Jackie, blue for Penny. Too stoned to speculate further, he slipped back into the kitchen where Rob was waiting, entranced, for the revelation of what was number eighteen in the chart.

Later, men with beards and women wearing too much eye make-up were swaying and shuffling, glasses held aloft, to the music in the sitting room, chipping away at conversation and hooting with intoxicated laughter. Over the course of the night, if previous years were anything to go by, the dancing was unlikely to become any more energetic, but the dancers would certainly shuffle closer together, if only for the purpose of holding each other up.

Rob and Tim were on the settee, a spliff passing back and forth between them. Rob had charge of a canister of scrumpy, held clamped between his knees; anyone requiring a refill was expected to pass him their empty glass. Phoenix dragged a dining chair over and straddled it backwards, folding his arms across the top of the chair's back. Rob passed him the joint and he took a long toke that burned the back of his throat.

Tim was watching out for a music teacher from Bristol called Liz, who he claimed to have knobbed in the bathroom at last year's party. He was hoping she'd be there again.

'How come you never mentioned it before?' Rob obviously thought Tim was making it up.

'I'd forgotten all about it until I was on my way here.'

'She's married,' said Phoenix.

Tim beamed with pride, as if that last snippet of information made his conquest all the more impressive.

'No, you wally. She just got married, a couple of months ago. JJ and Katy went to the wedding, so she'll probably have new hubby in tow this year.'

Tim shrugged his indifference. 'Perhaps he's crap in bed.'

Liz the music teacher (a frump in a purple velvet skirt that covered her ankles) arrived about ten minutes later, accompanied by a husband in the tweed jacket and green corduroy shirt that was the uniform of teachers of the more arty subjects. Phoenix saw Tim smile over at her, clearly convinced he was still in with a chance, but she didn't even bother to turn her head and look right through him and Phoenix gave him a triumphant told-you-so grin.

Meanwhile, Rob was ogling one of the Gingerbread mums. She was at least twenty-eight and was one of those women with long dirty hair who wore too much make-up and walked around with one hand deep in the front pocket of her jeans as if she couldn't go five minutes without feeling herself up. Phoenix was somewhat peeved when she used having met him before as an excuse to come and say hello, all the time flicking her false eyelashes in Rob's direction. Phoenix ignored her, and when she made a big show of going to the kitchen to get a drink, Rob wriggled himself free from the other sardines on the settee, handed over responsibility for the cider to Tim and followed after her. 'Need a piss,' he said.

'Bugger me,' said Tim. 'Shame he never moved that quickly on the rugby pitch at school.' He raised his glass at Rob's retreating back.

That was as much as Phoenix could take. If Rob - stoned, miserable Rob - could get off with someone that easily, Phoenix needed to take action. He dismounted

20

his chair and fought his way through the dancers. He clambered over the drinkers sitting on the stairs and barged into Penny's room to find Jackie and his sister sitting facing each other on the bed, cross-legged and giggling like morons.

His arrival wiped the smile from Penny's face.

'Piss off,' she hissed. Jackie turned and adjusted her grin to more of a Mona Lisa smirk, flirty and moist.

'Are you two lovebirds planning to come down and join the party? JJ and Katy want to know.'

'Come on, Pen, let's go and get another drink,' said Jackie, climbing off the bed and pulling Penny off with her. Jackie had changed into a short kilt that flicked up when she moved to reveal a pair of blue flowered knickers. Was she wearing knickers over her tights?

'Okay,' said Penny. 'Let's see if Marc and Dave are here.'

'Who?' said Phoenix, but the girls were already out of the door and halfway down the stairs.

Jackie's discarded hotpants lay in a squiggle of purple on the bed where she'd been sitting. He closed the door, crept over to the bed and buried his face in their warmth for a few seconds.

Phoenix found himself in the unpleasant position of being face to face, or at least chest to face, with David Browning, Katherine's boss and his own former English teacher. Browning, oblivious to his former pupil's haste to avoid him, started to witter about Oxford: 'So how about Matthias, is he still there? No, of course not, he must be long gone, must have been in his sixties when he taught me.' Phoenix muttered a cursory excuse me as he pushed past, and went to stand just inside the doorway of the sitting room where he could concentrate on more serious matters, specifically the movement of Jackie's kilt as she danced. Admittedly she wasn't the greatest dancer, the kilt had a better sense of rhythm than she did, but none of that mattered because the way the lamplight reflected on the smooth, taut tan of her leg as she shifted from one splayed stance to the next, was hypnotic.

For a moment he was reminded of Bambi on the ice, but then his brain registered that the rhythm of Jackie's leg movements had deteriorated entirely and that a minor commotion was in train as Penny was losing the fight to keep a putrid cocktail of cake and gin in her stomach. Penny pushed her friend away (from where Phoenix stood it looked as if Jackie was keeping a distance in any case), clamped a hand over her mouth and staggered, bent double, from the room, shoving people aside with her extended arm. Phoenix, sober enough to recognize the extent of his good fortune and pissed enough to take advantage of it, sauntered over to Jackie who had begun to jiggle again on the spot, looking guilty and apprehensive as though she had never been friendless in a social situation before.

'Shall we go and see if she's okay?' he said, grabbing her by the arm.

'Where did she go?'

'Upstairs to the bathroom.'

In fact, he was banking on Penny having made for the nearest toilet, the one outside, and on finding that to be occupied by Rob and his older woman having no option but to throw up in the garden. There was no time to lose. Phoenix ushered Jackie up the stairs, but not so close that he couldn't watch the swing of her kilt as she climbed.

Up on the landing he reached over her shoulder and rapped at the bathroom door. He turned the handle with one hand, grabbed Jackie's wrist with the other and pulled her into the bathroom with him, pushing the door shut with his back and locking them in with his free hand, keeping his back against the door in case she tried to escape.

Jackie's face feigned pantomime coyness. 'Where is she?' she said, glancing over her shoulder.

'Beats me. I could have sworn I saw her run up the stairs.'

'Perhaps she's in her room.'

'Nah, she's probably in the downstairs bog. How about a snog? As we're here.'

He still had hold of her wrist and pulled her in close so that she stumbled on her platforms. 'Dangerous things, platforms, can easily snap an ankle.'

'Why?' said Jackie.

'What do you mean, why?'

23

'Why do you want to snog me?'

'Because I fancy you, stupid, and you fancy me. So here's your big chance to look a gift horse in the mouth.'

'Piss off,' she said, staying put.

He tucked two fingers of his free hand into the waistband of her kilt and pulled her against his body. He clamped his mouth hard against hers and plunged his tongue against her teeth and on into the sweet-tasting recesses of her mouth. Her own taut tongue sought out his and engaged in battle but even then he could not relax, every nerve strained to keep her from pulling away. He pushed his hand further into the waistband until his fingers were fiddling with the top of her tights, but he couldn't reach far enough to locate the top of her pants. He prised her legs apart with his knee and slid his foot up the door for balance. It was going well; she was loving it.

He needed a free hand, but the force of letting go of the waistband might catapult her away from him even if she was happy to stay, which he still couldn't be confident of. He decided it was safe to let go of her wrist and with her newly liberated hand she did nothing more dangerous than push against the door to stop it rattling; another good sign. He pressed his knee harder into her crotch and she responded with a squeak of pleasure.

Encouraged, he shoved a hand against her belly and pulled at her blouse until he felt her skin under his palm, then headed north until he hit the soft, warm fabric of her

24

bra. His erection was prodding at his trousers; his hand rubbed at her breast, then he pulled it away again and guided her hand towards his fly. He knew she must be able to feel him trembling but it was too late to worry about that; his hand rubbed at her breast, then he pulled it away again and guided her hand towards his fly. He became aware of someone on the landing outside and froze. They both froze. It was Penny.

'Jackie? Jack?'

Phoenix gripped Jackie's wrist tighter and pressed his mouth harder against hers, but ultimately he knew that if Jackie wanted to be rescued there were any number of ways she could attract Penny's attention.

The doorknob turned one way then the other then Penny's voice called out: 'Sorry!' They waited, listening as she opened and closed the bedroom doors one by one, checking to see if Jackie had crashed out on one of the beds, too drunk to realize where she was.

At last she went away and Jackie pulled her brazen head away from Phoenix's and said, 'You can screw me if you like, but it'll be rape.'

'Now where did you learn a nasty word like that?' said Phoenix, and before she could answer, he covered her mouth with his own while his hand directed hers back towards his swollen cock. His other hand fumbled with his belt.

Together they unzipped his fly and he helped her to wrench his dick from the front of his pants. While she made tentative little taps against his foreskin with her fingers, he tugged at her tights. He located his target with his fingers, bent his knees like a diver preparing to spring and thrust himself up inside her. It wasn't easy getting in but she was wet, she was dripping, partly because he had come immediately.

His penis flopped out of her and he pulled away to grab a towel from the side of the bath. He wiped his dick first then handed her the towel to wipe herself while he put himself away. She turned away from him to wipe between her legs then handed him the towel. For good measure, he leaned over and gave her a quick peck on the cheek. 'Right,' he said. 'I'll go down first and you come down in a few minutes.' He unlocked the door and surveyed the landing and stairs, then dashed to his bedroom and threw the soiled towel under the bed from the doorway.

**

THE FOLLOWING FRIDAY, the evening before he was due to return to Oxford, Phoenix met Rob and Tim for a drink at the Rising Sun. Rob was dressed in his work clothes and was drenched in aftershave; he'd arranged to meet Jo - the woman he'd shagged at the party - at a club in town later and Tim was giving him a lift. Phoenix was setting off early the next morning, so Rob was the only one drinking. They left the pub at nine, with Phoenix

26

taking the lead on his bike and the other two following in Tim's Capri.

As Phoenix rounded the bend into Flax Bourton, the front of his helmet slipped down over his eyes. As he struggled one-handed to restore his vision, a gust of wind hit the front wheel of his bike, forcing him to swerve into the path of an oncoming van. The impact catapulted him back across the road. He bounced off the roof of the Tim's car and landed on the grass verge. He was dead even before he hit the Capri; the collision had broken his neck and cracked his helmet, driving a dagger-like shard of plastic into the soft flesh of his left temple.

The Show Must Go On

ON THE DAY OF PHOENIX'S FUNERAL, PENNY hated their mother. Not just because of her noisy, operatic sobbing: other people were doing that too (although Penny for some reason couldn't muster so much as a single tear and nor, she noticed, could her dad) but because, as usual, she was hogging the spotlight. Her eulogy was more like an audition piece for a bloody Shakespeare play. Someone should have told her it's no great achievement to upstage a dead person.

Penny tried distract herself by counting how many people were crying and how many weren't. At the beginning it had been pretty much even-stevens, but as Katherine dragged on, gulping as she struggled with each word, the criers definitely took the lead. Counting wasn't easy, what with Penny having been forced to sit sandwiched between her dad and the space Katherine would return to in the front row, meaning she had to keep twisting around to look. When she wasn't counting, she stared at the coffin, wondering if hers would be that long or if she would have shrunk by the time she died, as her grandparents seemed to be doing, as everyone did if you went by the seven ages of man poster in the school biology lab.

This was her first ever funeral; no one she knew had died before. Her gran and gramps, JJ's parents, were still alive and were there at Phoenix's funeral, stoic as ever, sitting to JJ's left. No one had ever met Katherine's parents, not even JJ, they didn't know Penny existed and if they ever knew Phoenix had been born, they had certainly not been told he was dead. And lucky them, not having to be there to witness their daughter's performance.

Even Jackie was crying. It was her first funeral too and she'd been sniffling, revving up, right from the beginning. Penny could tell it was her even without looking; recognized her crying voice even though she'd never heard her cry before. At least her grizzling meant she probably couldn't hear the drivel coming out of Katherine's mouth, so Penny could be grateful for one less thing to be embarrassed about.

She gave the room another quick sweep. It wasn't a proper church, more of a hexagonal brick bungalow with stained-glass windows; put up a mirror ball and it'd be a great place for a disco. When they'd first arrived, it had occurred to her to save a place for Phoenix, as if he had been held up at the petrol station or was travelling separately, on his stupid bike or with his stupid friends. As for his friends, all their faces were a weird grey colour, as if they were about to keel over themselves. Except Rob, whose face was beetroot, because

31

he was pissed or stoned or both at eleven o'clock in the morning. Or maybe he was embarrassed too.

Dead, dead, dead, Penny wanted to shout, just bloody say it. He's dead, not lost. How can you lose a six-foot-four nineteen-year-old? He's not lost, like a stupid coat button or your bloody car keys, he's *dead*!

Katherine fell silent, as if she'd heard Penny's thoughts, but more likely, Penny hoped, to signal the end of her eulogy. JJ breathed out, ever so slowly, as if he'd been trying to beat the *Guinness Book of Records* record for holding your breath at a funeral and failed.

Despite having finished, Katherine seemed reluctant to step down and return to her seat and just stood there, looking around as if she couldn't understand why no one was bloody clapping. Penny elbowed JJ in the ribs and at last he got up off his backside and fetched her, putting his arm around her shoulders and leading her back to her seat so that finally the music could start: Phoenix's favourite ever track of all time, 'Purple Spaceships Over Yatton' by Stackridge, the one record in his collection Penny didn't want to inherit, thanks all the same.

Penny slid her bum along the bench towards her gran so that her parents could sit together and so that she wouldn't be expected to comfort Katherine in public.

As soon as they sat down, the priest or vicar or whatever the hell he was if they weren't in a church looked shiftily around, not unlike the shoplifters who came into

Barker's, the stationery shop in Bristol where she worked on Saturdays. She noticed his arm move ever so slightly, no more than a twitch, as if he were dropping a stolen biro into his pocket, but instead he had pressed a button on the wall behind the coffin that triggered a buzz, then a jerk, followed by more jerks as the conveyor belt moved the coffin slowly away from them all, prompting more loud sobs from Katherine. A pretty clumsy exit, thought Penny, as a pair of red velvet curtains chased the coffin through to the other side, but that was Phoenix all over.

***

PENNY WAS STILL A VIRGIN at the age of fifteen and, being a six-foot-and-still-growing freak, was likely to stay that way throughout adulthood. Petite, properly proportioned Jackie wasn't, or at least claimed not to be. In fact she was adamant she had gone all the way with someone at the New Year's Eve party, but had so far refused to offer up any of the gory details. Since they'd spent most of the party together in Penny's room, Penny was tempted to call her a liar. Nevertheless she wasted hours in her room, reconstructing the highlights of that night, even though rehashing events already blurred by an overindulgence of gin and fairy cakes was never going to come to much.

But never mind the where-when-how of it, the who-the-hell-with of it was the big question Penny couldn't get her head around. There had been no decent boys at the party, or men for that matter, just her brother Phoenix and his gang of moronic mates, who'd spent most of the evening squashed onto the settee, too stoned or pissed to do anything but take the mickey out of whoever was brave or stupid or drunk enough to dance near them.

There'd certainly been no one bearing any resemblance to Marc Bolan, Jackie's idol who, she claimed, she had been saving herself for. So regardless of what Phoenix used to say about Jackie having a label saying Scrubber sewn into her knickers, there was no way it would have been Mr. Anyoldbugger-Justforthesakeofit. Penny knew her friend better than anyone, and she knew that if Jackie was unable to name her conqueror it must be due, in order of feasibility, to one of the following five conditions:

(1) As a new member of the Shagging Club, she was forbidden from revealing any information about the club or its membership, especially to a non-virgin;

(2) That she had shagged JJ's boss, the one with the Jason King moustache, and was now too embarrassed and ashamed to admit it;

(3) She was lying, and was still a virgin;

(4) She couldn't name whoever it was because they hadn't wasted any precious shagging time on trivialities like exchanging names; or

(5) She had been raped.

Penny's money was on (3), because what was the point

of losing your virginity at fifteen if you then refused to discuss it with your best mate? They'd both made up shagging stories often enough to know they had massive entertainment value, so maybe the answer was that Jackie was not clever enough to fabricate a whole story, complete with details, and was hoping that if she kept her mouth shut, Penny would give up and forget about it.

Subject exhausted, Penny's thoughts returned, as they did in every blank moment, to her brother Phoenix. She often forgot he had gone; only that morning she thought she had heard him shout OI, OUR SPROG from the other room as she sat eating her breakfast, and had ignored it as she always had. The irony was that if he were still alive he would be in Oxford and she wouldn't be missing him at all; in fact she would have been glad to see the back of him.

After the funeral she had wangled an extra week off school, while her parents had gone straight back to work in that Life Goes On kind of way that they applied to every crisis. On the face of it, not much had changed in the Jacobs household in the immediate aftermath of Phoenix's death; with the exception of one big difference. The bickering that was an a established feature of inter-parental communication had definitely got nastier. In the old days it would have gone something like this:

JJ: All right, so what's your concept of heaven? (They were always 'discussing' 'concepts' and bloody 'notions'.)

Katherine: Oooh-kaaay. An open expanse, perhaps a

35

long sandy beach like the one at Biarritz. Not a soul in sight, and no time restrictions.

JJ: So, what about nightfall? I suppose that doesn't count as a time restriction?

Katherine: No, just a signal that it's time to rest.

JJ: Then what about death? Surely that's the ultimate time restriction.

Katherine: Well, I rather thought that a prerequisite for admission to heaven was to be dead already.

Boom boom, as Basil Brush would say.

Since Phoenix's death, these so-called discussions had become spiked with an unpleasant overtone, and more often than not would end with JJ spending the evening in the Doghouse until after Katherine had gone to bed.

Whenever this happened, and it was happening with worrying frequency, Penny couldn't sleep until the light in the shed had gone off and she had lain in bed holding her breath and counting down - like they all had that night they'd sat in front of the TV waiting for Apollo 11 to splash into the Pacific Ocean - until she heard the rattle of the latch on the back door that signalled JJ's re-entry to the house. Even if he stayed out in the shed all day, it seemed important he returned to the house every night. And it was important, because one night he didn't. The light in the Doghouse went out, and Penny counted, but JJ didn't come in.

The morning after he didn't come in the night before he brought her a cup of tea in bed at the usual time, super-strong and over-sweet, which is how he seemed to think she liked it.

'It's that time again love,' he said, as he did every morning.

He was wearing the same clothes as the day before, which in itself was not that unusual, but his trousers were crumpled from not having been taken off and folded neatly over the back of the bedroom chair, and his collar-length hair was sticking out from behind his ears. His whole appearance had deteriorated to match the condition of his favourite writing jumper that had holes at the elbows and smelled of dead sheep because he wouldn't let anyone wash it. Something to do with the oils in the wool.

'You all right, Dad?' was as close as Penny could get to asking why he hadn't slept in the house.

'Fine thanks, love, but I'm a bit late this morning so you need to get a move on I'm afraid.'

Penny deduced that he'd fallen asleep at his desk by accident. She waited in her room, as she always did, until her mother had slammed the front door and reversed the Mini down the drive. She counted to thirty before going downstairs in case Katherine came back in, Columbo-style, as she often did to get something she'd forgotten.

The kitchen smelled of toast, which was normal. A plate and bowl waited at her place on the table, guarded by the cornflakes box and a bottle of milk. Normal. The daily loaf sat on the breadboard in the centre of the table, next to the candle that stayed there twenty-four hours a day in case of power cuts. Normal. The radio had been switched off to conserve its batteries. Very bloody annoying, but also normal.

She cut herself a doorstep and put it in the toaster to burn while she fetched a spoon from the draining board. It had been left to dry the wrong way up and had a tidemark in its bowl where the soapy water had dried in it (she'd always blamed Phoenix for that). Everything as usual. Life as it was normally lived.

It was Monday, JJ's deadline day, so he'd probably worked all night and fallen asleep at his desk, which was abnormal but allowable in the light of recent events. She left the house by the back door and banged her habitual rhythm on the Doghouse door as she passed.

'Bye love. Give those nuns hell,' he said, as he did every Monday morning.

The windows of the five-to-eight bus were steamed up with the combined breath of workers and shoppers on their way into town. Most of them had seen Penny get on the bus pretty much every morning for four years, but still found something worth staring at. She screwed up her nose and headed for her usual double seat near the back, plonked her bag down to save the seat next to her and counted the three stops until Jackie got on.

As they passed through the village she rubbed at the window and scowled out at the horde of Comprehensive-goers queuing for the free coaches to ferry them in the opposite direction; to the school Phoenix had gone to, the school Penny would have chosen to go to if their mother didn't work there.

''Right our Pen?'

''Right our Jack?'

'Where were you on Saturday? I popped in to see you.'

'Where, at home?' People were always dropping into the Jacobs house unannounced, especially Phoenix's mates, and Penny didn't want Jackie to start doing it too.

Jackie was lucky; the Benhams lived on the new estate in the village, in a neat square box of a house with windows that closed properly in winter. The front of their house was open on to the street, no walls or broken trellises or scruffy hedges, just a rectangle of grass that Jackie's dad could mow during halftime on a Saturday afternoon and a short tarmac driveway that swept under the car port attached to the side of the house. At the back, another shorn green oblong was home to a tortoise with the name PERKY painted in white on its shell (Jackie didn't cry when PINKY died). Jackie's house had wall-to-wall carpets in every room, and a tropical fish tank that buzzed in the lounge. Her mum, Lesley, wore a flowerdy (as Jackie pronounced 'flowery') housecoat on her days off and kept the house spotless. She wore nail varnish and had her hair done once a week and said flip and sugar instead of bugger and shit. Jackie's dad worked for Hollings's Insurance, drove a new Morris Marina and spent his Saturday mornings at the golf course while the girls were out shopping.

'No, you dildo, at the shop. You know, that place you go on a Saturday to nick stuff.'

'Shut up. I don't nick stuff. I wasn't there anyway. They made me take a few weeks off.'

'See, they're on to you. They've noticed that the takings go up when you're not there and they're going to give you the sack. I got a pair of those new hotpants, the ones with the bib.'

'Lucky cow. What colour did you get?'

'Purple.'

'Nice. You've already got a purple pair.'

'I've gone off those.'

Jackie and her mum went shopping together every Saturday. In the Jacobs household the Benhams had been denounced by Katherine as a 'modern consumerist' family; they spent their free time in ways that Penny's mother wouldn't dream of. Jackie's mum was younger than Katherine and dressed like Jackie's glamorous older sister while Katherine dressed like a hippy at a job interview. It struck Penny that being a modern consumer was more bloody fun than anything Katherine ever did. For starters it was about spending money on things like clothes and records and holidays instead of textbooks and outings and theatre trips and 'travel'.

Penny liked to compare. Life at Jackie's house was clean, neat and effortless. No one was ever grumpy (except Jackie of course), there was always a choice of cereals on the breakfast table and they ate sliced white bread and frozen vegetables. They bought cheese straws ready-made from the supermarket. Their daily newspaper of choice was the *Bristol Evening Post*, which they read because it was small and neat and certainly not because they were fans of Penny's dad's column. In fact, they probably didn't even know who John Jacobs was, let alone that he was Penny's father. If they did read it, they wouldn't agree with anything in it.

All the Benhams were of average height, they wore average-sized shoes that lined up neatly in the hallway. Their clothes were washed in an automatic twin-tub and dried on a rotary washing line, and they had a push-button trimphone in avocado, which they pronounced *aDvocado*. Jackie was neat and glossy with a smooth ponytail the colour of honey and her school uniform was washed and ironed twice a week by her mother. And as soon as a hole appeared in her American Tan tights they were thrown away and replaced by a new pair. The Benhams weren't rich; they just spent their money wisely.

'Wake up our Pen, we're yere.'

'Bloody'ell our Jack, that were quick.'

That's how they spoke to each other, to set themselves apart from the posh girls, only Jackie had to exaggerate less than Penny.

They walked from the bus stop to the school gates, to join the stream of maroon that flowed slow as a tart's spilled nail polish towards the ivy-covered school entrance.

'Right, so what's your bet for today?' said Penny.

'Snot'n'bogey pie, followed by frogspawn,' said Jackie.

'Okay. So, I'm going for tubes wrapped in liver with sprouts and mash, followed by chocolate pudding with mint custard.'

'You're on,' said Jackie.

'No I'm not,' said Penny in mock indignation.

''Right our Pen.'

''Right our Jack.'

And, because they were in different streams for most subjects, they parted company until lunch.

When it came to the first course they were both miles out. It was fish and chips. Not fish and chips like you buy from the chippy, but not a bad imitation either. The chips were drier, so was the fish, probably because they had been cooked at ten and left sitting around in the school kitchen until lunchtime. But it was still recognizable as fish and chips, and accompanied by mushy peas so green you were in danger of getting radiation sickness if you so much as looked at them. Penny was closest on the pudding, because she'd mentioned the word chocolate, but was still wrong: Australian crunch with chocolate custard.

Two palatable courses at the same meal? The girls suspected an ulterior motive; perhaps a terrible announcement was in the offing. *I'm sorry girls, but it turns out Mary was not a virgin after all, and Sister Dementia has fainted and had to be taken to the hospital.* Shock bloody horror. Penny pretended to shield her eyes as she shovelled up a forkful of nuclear peas. Which reminded her. 'Oh no,' she said. 'I've got History next.'

'Uh oh, we're all doomed,' said Jackie, in an unidentifiable accent.

Penny's History teacher, Mrs Bassett - in theory one of the few non-virgin teachers on the staff at St. Bernadette's, although anyone looking at her would doubt it - was obsessed by nuclear war. Hours of valuable teaching time had been expended in persuading her class that World War Three was guaranteed to kick off some time in the next twenty years and would wipe out anyone without access to the underneath of a sturdy dining table. Their O-level textbook showed photographs of charred tree stumps in Japan, and an artist's impression of a 'nuclear' family standing hand in hand and inexplicably naked (rear view only of course), staring into the distance at the mushroom cloud that would be doing for them in the not-so-distant future.

When the Arab-Israeli war started the year before, Penny's gran had agreed with Mrs Bassett and insisted that the next world war would begin in the Middle East, scaring Penny stiff. She had been on constant red alert ever since so that even the theme tune of the evening news had taken on the significance of a three-minute warning, compelling her to leave the sitting room whenever it came on the television. So convinced was she that her end was

43

nigh that where once there had been clouds in the shape of rabbits and giraffes she saw only giant mushrooms, and when Phoenix died she couldn't help thinking he was well out of it. Why Our Lord had selected him and not her as the one to escape the great fry-up was a mystery though; if Phoenix had possessed any saintly qualities he had kept them well hidden. It was Penny who had been martyred on the cross of Catholic girls' school by her atheist mother, so why not take her?

The other girls in her class made light of Mrs Bassett's apocalyptic fixation, using it to instigate endless debate about how they would spend their last three minutes on this earth. Having sex with a pop star was the obvious consensus. But for Penny, at those times, when she came to thinking that she would never find a boyfriend before the three-minute warning sounded and was destined to die a virgin, or when her parents' so-called 'discussions' focused on all the terrible and frightening things going on in other parts of the world, she would sit up in her room and wish for it all to be over, for whatever was going to happen to happen right then. Perhaps then there might be a chance for the world to start again. Preferably without the person who had discovered how to split the atom.

Of late though Mrs Bassett had been suffering the odd fleeting distraction, such as the introduction of the three-day week, and one day she had suggested that in twenty-five years (when Penny would be forty) nobody would work a full week, that all jobs would be shared and that they would all have to understand the importance of the constructive use of leisure time or else risk an outbreak of national boredom of epidemic proportions, which would in turn lead (obviously) to widespread violent crime.

Not naturally one for drawing unnecessary attention to herself, Penny was so outraged at the contradiction of this statement in the context of her teacher's usual obsessions that she propelled her arm into the air and, without waiting for the nod, called out: 'But Miss, I thought you said we would all be dead by then,' and at home she had received lavish praise, particularly from JJ, for her ability to spot and challenge such a gross contradiction, even though it had been a simple exercise in addition. But at school her punishment was to read a book by John Hersey called - guess what - *Hiroshima*, and to write a one-page review of it during detention to be read out in class.

But that day, the day of fish and chips and Australian crunch, the day JJ didn't come in the night before, Mrs Bassett was away. A rumour claiming to stem from an eyewitness account had her being bundled into the back of an ambulance by men in white coats and whisked off to the funny farm, but Sister Clare, who stood in for her and clearly knew nothing about history because she got them all to sit quietly and read from their textbooks, said she had a touch of the 'flu. Consequently, Penny had nothing interesting to report when she met Jackie in the library at the end of the day.

45

''Right our Jaaaaack?'

''Right our Peeeeeen?'

They sat in silence for a few moments until Penny, restless for intrigue, declared for the umpteenth time that she knew who it was Jackie had shagged on New Year's Eve.

Jackie sighed. 'No you don't,' she said.

The librarian intervened with a sharp shush from behind her desk and Penny lowered her voice. 'Yes I do, I've worked it out.' Since Penny had resigned herself to the idea that Jackie was lying, her strategy for annoying Jackie into truthful submission was to come up daily with more and more ridiculous suggestions until she gave in.

'Who is it now?' said Jackie.

'Alan Watts, my dad's boss.'

'What?'

'No, *Wattssss*, Alan, works at the paper. He was at the party. Thinks he looks like Jason King off the telly. You know who I mean, you like him, I saw you staring at him.'

'Fuck off, you didn't. Look, Pen, stop going on about it, I wish I never mentioned it. Let me get on with this or I'll have to do it at home.'

'Ooh, sorry Miss Stropknickers. Have you got an important essay to write, a pressing deadline to meet?'

Jackie raised a smile at last but Penny interpreted her failure to laugh out loud as an indication that perhaps it hadn't been such a wild guess after all. The awful thought occurred that maybe the right answer was a combination of options number (2) and (5) and that Jackie had been raped, because why else would she refuse point blank to talk about it? JJ's boss was a right creep with his Triumph Stag and his velvet jackets, she wouldn't put it past him to rape someone. Nobody in their right mind would shag him voluntarily. Penny watched Jackie's pen scratch loops and swirls across the page of her exercise book, and another thought struck her; not for the first time if she were entirely honest, but this time the thought wouldn't budge, insisted on having a shot at the big prize. 'Jack?' Jackie grunted but didn't look up.

'It wasn't our Phoenix, was it?'

Jackie stopped and lifted her head, and all the golden light had gone from her face, and Penny knew she'd guessed right this time.

'Fuckinell Jack.'

'If you two can't work quietly, you'll have to leave.' The librarian issued her ultimatum in a fierce whisper that sprayed the surface of their table with minuscule gobbets of saliva. On any other day this would have would have led to them being ejected in fits of giggles and spending the entire journey home inventing new nicknames for the librarian like Pledgemouth or Gobber. But on the day in question, the day of fish and chips, Australian crunch, JJ sleeping in the shed and Jackie having shagged Penny's dead brother, Jackie packed her things into her brown leather satchel without so much as raising her eyes to look at Penny, who hadn't even unfastened her bag and so had nothing to do but wait. Jackie hitched one strap over her shoulder and Penny followed her to the door.

They walked to the bus stop in silence and in silence they took their seats next to each other when the bus came. Jackie spent the whole journey staring out of the window at the smog until Long Ashton post office when she squeezed past Penny and got off the bus without looking back or waving or anything, not even so much as a V-sign.

Penny sat on Phoenix's bed, something she would never have been allowed to do without permission if he were still alive, even if he were away at college. He would have killed her for calling it 'college', too. She picked at the tufts of his candlewick with her fingernails, plucking them out to reveal a precise row of little holes, the first line of a tiny R at the beginning of the word RAPIST. Her own bedspread, identical but for the colour (apricot, his was light blue), had PENNY plucked out of it in a similar fashion. It would take hours, but she was prepared to sacrifice whatever time it took to get the point across to her brother. So there she sat, defacing his bedspread and calling it college, hoping he could see her and read her thoughts, because at that point in time she hated his guts and he couldn't do anything about any of it.

She stood up to inspect her work from a distance then, satisfied it couldn't be seen by anyone but herself, scanned the bed, the floor, the walls, for evidence of the evil deed. Supposing they had done it right there on that very bed, where she'd been sitting?

His room, which he had complained about at Christmas for being too empty (because most of his stuff had been carted off to Oxford), was cluttered with all the boxes and bags of his junk, untouched since they'd brought them all home two days after the funeral. What would they do with his stuff when they finally got round to sorting it out? Penny was looking forward to Katherine finding his collection of porn mags.

She was furious with Jackie, not for not telling her sooner, but because her having slept with her brother gave her some claim over his death which, when it came to Penny's life outside the Jacobses' house, had been her tragedy alone. Jackie's revelation had somehow made it hers too. There were many things that she would happily share with her best friend; her homework, a bottle of scrumpy, her new brown eyeshadow, even her brother if he were alive. But her memories of him were hers to share with no one and she didn't want Jackie worming her way into the picture.

If Phoenix hadn't died there was a chance she might have been pleased to discover her best friend had lost her virginity to him, would have relished the potential for months of teasing. But Phoenix's death had cancelled out any fun to be had from the situation and the thought of the two of them together made her queasy. Phoenix's legacy to

Jackie was a stain in her knickers and perhaps the unspoken promise of another shag at some other party, a promise that had been broken by fate but probably, knowing Phoenix, would have been broken anyhow. Penny couldn't trust Jackie not to try to make more of it than that and find some way of gatecrashing her own misery. Scrubber.

A rhythmic grating noise that she recognised to be the sound of a retching cat interrupted her thoughts. Both cats were on her bed. By the time she made it to her room, Wedgie had deposited a neat cylinder of bile-coated fur onto her candlewick. She looked up at the ceiling. 'One all,' she said.

Something was really up with JJ, because when she went down to return the Dettol to the kitchen he asked her to switch off the news and keep him company in the sitting room. If they'd just announced the outbreak of global conflict and he was about to break it to her gently, he was in for a shock because she didn't care any more. As it turned out he was tired and wanted her to chat to him to keep him awake until dinnertime. That was her cue to ask him why he had slept out in the shed, but she knew his explanation would amount to a frustrating babble of half-truths about being behind with his work and blah blah bloody blah. So instead she yacked on about Jackie's mum's new job to fill the time until dinner.

At the dinner table Penny looked across at her brother's empty chair and pledged never to invite Jackie for tea again because if she did she would have to sit there and that would be much too creepy. Besides, Katherine had taken to eating meals with her coat on and hardly speaking at all.

'Did you get your column finished, Dad?'

'Just about.'

'What's it about? As if we didn't know,' said Penny.

'Idi Amin's Save Britain Fund. Do you know they had a goat auction in Uganda and raised three hundred pounds for the fund? And Amin said if Britain goes hungry that he'll send us bananas. So we've no need to worry.'

'God. What on earth will you find to write about when everything's back to normal?' said Penny, forgetting that 'normal' and 'abnormal' were two of her parents' favourite discussion triggers.

This was just the kind of question that in ordinary circumstances would be the starting pistol for an enthusiastic philosophical debate on the concept of normality that would send Penny scrambling for the door as soon as she had finished eating. Not this time. Katherine and JJ locked eyes for a moment, then Katherine hissed at Penny to be quiet.

The only sound during the rest of the meal was that of the serving spoon ringing against the side of the Pyrex dish as Penny helped herself to seconds. And in the end it was Penny who broke the dumb silence by putting down her cutlery and complimenting JJ on his cooking to cheer him up. 'Not bad, Dad. You've given up trying to kill us all off, then?' At which point, Katherine dropped her knife

51

and fork, which was loaded with food, onto her plate.

Penny and JJ turned expectant faces in her direction as if she had dinged on her glass with the edge of her knife before making an important announcement, but, as Penny had suggested, these were abnormal times and instead she scraped her chair backwards, pulled her coat tight around her body and stormed out of the room and it was all action stations as JJ went grovelling after her with a hot-water bottle.

'Clear the table love,' he said as he left the room.

'Doesn't anyone say please and thank you around here any more?' But she did as she was told, as noisily as possible to avoid having to listen to whatever was going on upstairs and after about five minutes JJ came back.

'Is she all right?'

'Yes, she's having a lie-down,' he said.

Penny's parents never had a lie-down on their own. Phoenix used to say that whenever their parents had argument they were building up to sex, and whenever they went out to the Doghouse together they were going to have sex, out there in the cold and filth. Talk about one-track mind. If he'd been right, he'd well and truly put paid to it now. But something good must have happened because JJ had perked up a bit. He flapped the tea towel over his arm, saying: 'You wash and I'll dry, and chop, chop, the *Panorama* election special starts in ten minutes.'

'Oh god,' said Penny. 'Do we have to?'

'It's history in the making,' he said, adopting the same tone he would use to tempt her with a box of Quality Street. 'You'll remember this time when you're older as an important U-turn in social history. The people coming together to bring down an incompetent government, it's what democracy should be all about. Setting great precedents.'

'No thanks Dad, I'm tired. I think I'll have an early night.'

When the washing-up was done, she kissed him goodnight and went up to her room to listen to records, keeping the volume down low so as not to give Katherine any reason to come in.

Penny's main Christmas present from her parents had been a stereo music centre: teak base, smoky lid, integrated tape cassette and two separate speakers. Phoenix had set it up for her, using a tape measure to position the speakers at an equal distance away from the mother ship, as he called it, for the full stereo effect. He'd put one on the dressing table and the other on the bookcase, where they still were. Never one to let such an opportunity slip by, he attached to her present a debt of gratitude to himself, to be repaid at an unspecified date, by reminding her that it was a much better present than if he hadn't persuaded the parents to let him have a motor bike. A debt that Penny had now been let off. At the time she had told him to piss off less nastily than usual because it was Christmas, and now she was glad she had because he was probably right.

She pulled an old copy of *Jackie* from the pile stored under her bed and flicked through, stopping to inspect a close-up of Marty Kristian, who she quite fancied in secret but could never admit to fancying openly because he was too clean-cut for *Jackie's* tastes. Or was he? Now Jackie had shagged Phoenix there was no telling who she might fancy, or if she had any taste in boys at all. She changed into her nightie and went to brush her teeth in the bathroom. On the way back to her room she put her ear to her parents' bedroom door. Should she go and wish Katherine goodnight? Better not.

She lay in bed in the dark, too tired to read and too wakeful to sleep. The back door creaked as JJ put the cats out for the night. She waited for the sound of his footsteps on the stairs, but instead she heard the crunch of his slippers on the gravel path and the rattle of the latch on the Doghouse door. She held her breath for a few moments and counted, perhaps he had gone out to fetch something or to switch something off, but when she'd got to one hundred and there'd been no reverse procedure, she sat up and pulled back the curtain.

The light in the shed was on and its stretched reflection on the lawn flickered with her father's shadow as he moved around. There was no excusing his spending a second night out there. If he was behind with his work he could have not spent the whole evening watching television. Something terrible was happening.

***

KATHERINE WOUND THE CAR WINDOW down a fraction to let in some air and clear the condensation from the windscreen; even such a minor exertion exhausted her, yet in a few minutes she would have to summon...BANG! A hand slammed against the window at her right ear. A big hand, so close she could predict its owner's future. Then the door yanked open, the cold air almost sucking her out of the car. Jesus. Ray Perkins.

'Mornin', he said. After years of shouting at children over the grind of lathes, his voice was a fair impersonation of a tanker coming in to dock at Avonmouth. He flashed his tobacco-stained teeth too close to her face; his breath smelled like a pub carpet.

'Jesus, Ray, you made me jump.'

'You coming in or what?'

'Just gathering my thoughts, Ray.'

'Don't suppose any of 'em involve me?'

'Funnily enough, Ray, they don't.'

'More's the pity.'

Ray Perkins, woodwork teacher, happily married and a bit of the one with the ladies. That's how he told it in any case, because as far as Katherine knew, none of the 'ladies' he encountered on a daily basis - Katherine being one of them - could testify to any level of prowess in the seduction stakes. But he did draw you in, in an 'us teachers of marginalized, namby-pamby arts subjects must stick together you know' kind of way.

'Come on,' he said. 'Race you to the staffroom.'

'Oh god. I'm really not up to running this morning. I'll see you in there.'

'Right you are my lover, I'll get the kettle on. How many sugars again?'

Jesus, Ray, she wanted to shout. Please just bugger off and leave me alone. 'Two, please.'

'See you in there then,' he said, and slammed her door shut with such force it immediately sprang open again.

Katherine rested her head against the steering wheel. Was there nowhere she could find any peace? She counted to ten, sucked in some Perkins-violated air, rewound the window and pulled her briefcase onto her lap. First lesson was the fourth-year CSE group. Life just got more and more cruel.

In the staffroom, Ray was waiting with the institutional standard ridged cup and saucer, insipid jade in colour. Proof that the tea had been sugared and stirred was in the cluster of tiny bubbles rocking in the vortex created by the spoon.

'Here you go my lover, want a biccy? Got some nice suggestives, good dunkers.'

In keeping with his occupation, Ray preferred even his biscuits to be made of sawdust.

'Thanks Ray, just the tea's great, I've not long since had breakfast.'

As fortune would have it, Ray, ever a man with a contingency plan, had in any case lined up another 'lady' to share his biscuits with.

The staffroom was busy but quiet, save the odd rattle of cup against saucer, the rustle of newspaper pages being turned, the occasional expletive as a biscuit held too long in tea disintegrated into a soggy mess; at least they had the decency to ignore her. Not one person had been brave enough to remove their coat; the heating had been off all weekend to save fuel and would take at least a day to crank itself up again.

She chose an empty chair between two teachers she didn't know too well and who wouldn't expect her to engage in dreaded small talk, but whose proximity might warm her a little. But before she could lower herself down someone touched her right elbow.

'Katherine?' David Browning, head of English, Katherine's immediate boss.

'Morning, David.'

No peace.

'Can I nab you for a minute?' He nodded his head towards the door. He might have allowed her a few minutes to drink her tea, but he meant right away. 'Bring your tea,' he said.

Katherine followed him into an empty classroom. David perched himself on the desk at the front of the room, legs spread to reveal a small hole in the crotch of his trousers through which shone a sixpence of white Y-front.

He gestured to her to take a seat in front of him.

'I'm okay standing, thanks,' she said. 'What's up?'

'Nothing to worry about,' he said. Lack of concern was always a bad sign with him. 'Just that I had a quick word with the Head on Friday, and he's agreed that if you need it -' (he emphasized the 'if' by pressing his hand down on his knee) '- it would be okay to reorganize the English staff to cover the Drama syllabus. Only if you need it, mind, there's no pressure on you, I just want you to know it's there if you -' (press, spread) '- need it.'

'Thank you, David, but I'm fine,' she said. 'I'd rather keep myself busy.'

'Well, just let me know, all right? Here's my home phone number, just in case.' He handed her a slip of paper from his jacket pocket, the same jacket he had worn, day in and day out, since she had first joined the department eight years ago; green and brown dogtooth check with a huge red stain in the corner of the pocket in question. 'Call any time.'

'Yes, thank you.'

David slid down from the table onto his short legs. 'Come on,' he said. 'Your tea's getting cold.'

He left her at the staffroom door. She drained her cup in one go, out there in the corridor rather than suffer the atmosphere of the staffroom a second time, and took the cup and saucer to her classroom to sit out the minutes until the bell would summon her to Assembly.

She was home early that day, just before four. The power was out and the house was in darkness. She felt her way through to the kitchen, where it was warm thanks to the Aga, and the smell of bacon still lingered from JJ's lunch. From the window she could see the flicker of his gas lamp out in the Doghouse. The matches were on the kitchen table, next to the candle. She struck one and lit it. The tea on the stove had been recently topped up; she took a cup from the draining board and filled it.

She took the matches through to the sitting room and lit the ends of newspaper that poked out from beneath the pile of kindling and logs in the grate.

She pulled her favourite armchair in close to the hearth, wrapped her sheepskin coat tighter around her body and clamped it to her with folded arms. Thank god for sheep.

She settled down to watch the flames and wait for the next wave of grief to hit.

The light came on.

'Sorry, Mum, were you asleep?'

'Must have dropped off,' said Katherine. 'Damn, the fire's gone out. Bloody miners.'

'How come it's their fault?'

'If we had coal, it would burn longer. At least the power's back on. I'll make tea in a minute. How was school?'

'Rubbish.'

'Oh well, at least it's no longer boring. Do you have any homework?'

'Done it. Me and Jack stayed on in the library.'

'Jackie and I.'

'Jackie's mum's got a new job. International Secretary.'

'Oh, very glamorous. Will she get to travel?'

'I don't know, but she's going to learn Esperanto.'

'Hmm, that should come in useful.'

'MUM!'

Katherine sighed. 'What shall we have for supper?' Too late, Penny had raised the drawbridge.

'Not hungry.'

Everything as usual.

'I'm going up to my room,' said Penny.

'Please will you sort the fire out before you go?'

Penny tutted, but threw her bag down on the floor and set about replacing the charred foundations of the fire.

'Have you thought any more about staying on at school?'

'Not really. Jackie's going to leave and train to be an air hostess.'

'Oh dear.'

'What's that supposed to mean?'

'Nothing, I'd just hoped she was a bit brighter than that. I suppose it doesn't matter what you start off doing. As long as you have some idea of what you want to do with your life before you start having children. It doesn't do to start a family too young.'

'You did.'

'I wasn't that young, and I knew what I wanted to do.'

'What, be a teacher?'

'Well, work with theatre in some way. Actually I wanted to be a playwright.'

'Did you? How come you never mentioned it before?'

'I don't know, I must have forgotten.'

'So what's the point of knowing what you want to do, if you go and forget what it was until you're too old to do anything about it? You're bonkers. I'm going upstairs.'

Katherine stared at the tiny hole, held in check with pink nail varnish, on Penny's American Tan thigh, exposed as she rocked back onto her haunches to haul herself up from the hearth. Then it was gone, covered by the maroon drop of her skirt.

She sat on her bed and lowered her head into her hands, as she might instruct a fainting teenager, lifted from Assembly, to do. Her palms were numb as if drained of blood. All her energy had leaked away and now all that remained was the faint glimmer of a will to survive as she gulped down each breath. If her concentration wavered from the complicated process of breathing, even for a split second, she would die. She raised her head. The dressing table seemed to have shifted further away from her; if she were to try to reach it, it would not be where her eyes told her it was and she would tumble on to the carpet.

The sound of a door closing somewhere shifted her

attention. Phoenix? No, of course not. It was the door next to his she had heard, and those were Penny's footsteps on the landing. Katherine sat up straight and gave a little cough that said: I'm in here so please knock before you come in. But Penny crossed the landing and onto the stairs without stopping. Phoenix would have come in, cough or no cough.

Her breathing was regular again. She patted the bedspread; how she would have loved to crawl into bed, pull back the sheets, lower her head into the soft nest of the pillow and release into that same oblivion she had been fighting so hard to resist. But the bedside clock showed twenty past six, she had missed the six o'clock news and the remains of her family would be waiting for its tea. It was time to go down.

The TV was off and JJ was sitting in her armchair, with Penny on the rug in front of the fire wittering on again about Jackie's mother's new job. Katherine made a brief stop in the doorway to ask Penny to set the table and continued through to the kitchen. Penny clomped in and rattled around in the cutlery drawer, looking over her shoulder as she pulled the shepherd's pie from the oven. 'Doesn't look bad for one of Dad's efforts, does it?' she said.

'Let's eat before it gets cold.'

'Dad! It's on the table!'

JJ and Penny rabbited on over dinner about Idi Amin and his fucking bananas and what they would do when life returned to normal, as if the death of a son and brother were no more than a temporary inconvenience, like a wet day on a camping trip. It was more than she could stand.

'For god's sake, shut up!'

She'd said it out loud, and for a few minutes there was peace, but then Penny made a stupid joke about JJ trying to kill them all with his cooking and it hit her again, the thought that had been nagging at her for weeks. Phoenix's death was JJ's fault. *He* had helped to persuade her, Katherine, that buying a motor bike was a good idea, *he* had bought a crash helmet in the wrong size, *he* had sent him out on the road alone before he was ready. In her rush to escape, Katherine upended her chair and stumbled towards the stairs.

She dithered on the landing, unable to decide which room would provide the most privacy, bathroom or bedroom. Downstairs, someone was scraping the remains of their dinner into the bin, and someone else was filling the kettle. Carrying on as normal. She pushed her way into the bathroom, locked the door and perched her backside down on the edge of the bath. Her head was starting to ache; there was aspirin in the cabinet but she hadn't the energy to get up again. In the distance, the kettle's whistle screeched to a climax then died away. Katherine moved her feet and studied their ghostly imprint on the bathmat.

Quick footsteps on the stairs. Not Penny's. Now on the landing. A faint rap at the door, the wrong door, and a timid: 'Katherine?' She heard him open their bedroom door and go in. A few moments later he crossed the landing again and she heard him open and close the door to Phoenix's room. He knocked at the bathroom door.

'Go away. Leave me alone.'

'I thought you might like a hot-water bottle. I've put it in the bed.'

'Please leave me alone.'

'Katherine, talk to me.' He was loud-whispering.

'No. I can't talk to you any more. You killed my son.'

'Katherine, let me in. I don't want Penny to hear this.'

'She's not stupid. You heard what she said as well as I did. She knows you killed him.'

'Penny doesn't know any such thing, and that wasn't what she meant, you know that. Kathy, I can see how you've come to think the way you do, but you know it's not true, I know you do. You're grieving. We all are.'

'Don't tell me what I know. Go away. I want my son back.' Katherine's words wavered as they forced their way up through the constricted pipe of her throat.

After one last desperate, despondent '*Kathy*', JJ shuffled his feet and after a bit went downstairs.

It wasn't until Penny had banged up the stairs and into her room that Katherine emerged from the bathroom and went into the bedroom. The hard edge of the bath had dug ridges into the backs of her thighs. Stopping only to prise off her shoes, she climbed into bed still wearing her coat. The hot-water bottle had been placed at shoulder level, where she usually liked it. She pushed it away towards her feet.

Katherine was already awake when JJ brought her a cup of tea, but she kept her eyes closed. You smell, was all she could think of to say by way of thanks, but kept it to herself for fear it might be taken the wrong way, as an invitation to be attacked by JJ's tickling fingers. And she probably didn't smell too great herself having passed a restless night in her coat.

He didn't hang around, and when he had gone she rolled herself out of bed. Pleated skirts were not designed to withstand the kind of treatment hers had been subjected to overnight and one side of it had flattened out completely. Her tights were twisted around her legs and her sweater smelled of B.O.

She set about dismantling herself and rebuilding a person more suited to the demands of the day ahead. She draped fresh clothes - striped blouse, green cord midi skirt, brown cardigan - over the radiator to warm, wrapped herself in JJ's dressing gown and headed for the bathroom. No sign of life yet from Penny's room, no smell of burning toast from the kitchen. At this time in the morning, the house was all hers.

In the kitchen, the cats had been fed, the breakfast table laid, the tea was on the stove and JJ had made himself scarce. A day like any other. Never had she been so grateful for a day like any other. Except it wasn't.

Too exhausted to eat, she poured herself a fresh cup of tea, adding an extra spoonful of sugar to wake herself up. The sitting-room fire had been swept out and relaid. What would have to happen to JJ for him to abandon his good elf routine?

The clock on the mantelpiece showed seven twenty-five: Penny should be getting up and Katherine should be leaving. She switched on the kitchen radio to kill the silence, tuning it to Radio One as a signal to Penny, but as soon as she did the batteries faded and she had to haul herself up the stairs again to tap at Penny's door.

'Are you up? Can I come in?'

A grunt, which she took for permission to enter. Katherine opened the door wide and peered into the darkened room. 'I'm off now. Shall I open your curtains?'

'No thanks. I'm getting up.' Penny stretched her bare arms above her head by way of illustration.

'All right then, I'll see you later. Have a good day at school.'

'You too Mum, see you later.' Penny rolled onto her side, arms disappearing back under the blankets.

'Penny, you'll be late!'

'Okay Mum, bye.'

Katherine fetched her coat from her bedroom floor, where Benn had curled up on it to sleep. She shook him off and attempted to brush away any loose hairs before putting it on, sniffing it to check he hadn't peed on it. That cat liked to wee in any spare nook and cranny it could find; it wouldn't be the first time she had gone to school smelling of cat's pee.

As she changed down into third for the bend at Flax Bourton, the bend where Phoenix had died, she heard Jim Morrison's voice growling over and over in her head about the end. She switched on the radio to drown it out and drove on past neat suburban bungalows connected to the road by long steep driveways. These were the homes of the children she taught, the intelligent, boxed-in children she taught. Another half mile and she would be there, at school, expected to perform.

She approached the bend that obscured the right-hand turn into the school car park but the fingers of her right hand didn't flick the indicator arm, nor did her left foot depress the clutch nor her left hand reach out to manoeuvre the gear stick into third and then second position to make the turn. A brief glimpse of Ray Perkins' grey Maxi as she sailed by, too quickly to establish if he was sitting there waiting for her. Well he would have a long wait.

If a sense of euphoria was missing from her actions it was because they were being committed without thought, and certainly without premeditation. She kept on driving out of necessity: over the crossroads, up past the Rising Sun, out of the village towards Brockley Combe and on.

Two miles short of Weston-Super-Mare she ran out of petrol. Yes, the orange petrol light had been flashing, and yes the engine had made sucking noises and juddered in warning, but she had paid those signs as much attention as she had the passing hedges and fields. In the engine's dying moments, she managed to steer the car in and bump its passenger side wheels onto the pavement. She dragged her briefcase from the foot well and set off to continue her journey on foot, as if she knew where she was going, as if she had sat down with a map before setting out and planned a route towards a specific destination.

She turned the collar up on her coat, clasped her briefcase to her chest for extra protection against the cold, and began walking. She set herself a target. The little café with the red plastic tablecloths that she and Phoenix had once stopped at for tea after his cross-country competition, where she could warm her hands on a mug of tea and feel better. She traipsed on through the cold, towards that distant beacon that would keep her alive, its imagined warm glow blotting her bleak horizon with a single spot of colour. When she arrived, she took a few deep breaths to summon the willpower to push against the door and go in.

A bell jangled on its wire above her head. Inside, her imagined beacon was more like a furnace. The air was stuffy and thick with cigarette smoke. The faces, the tablecloths and tomato-shaped ketchup containers, plastic chairs scraped back on lino, were in all shades of red. A purple-faced man turned to look up at her and his broad West Country accent puttered from one corner of his mouth. A cigarette dangled from the other side and jiggled up and down as he spoke.

'Shut door love, you'm letting all th'eat out.'

Katherine shut the door and the bell rang again.

'What can I get you my lover?' shouted the auburn-haired woman through a cloud of steam that puffed out of the still.

'Tea, please.' The sound of her own voice boomed

inside her head. She chose a chair in what she hoped would be the coolest part of the café, next to the window which glittered with condensation.

'One tea coming up.'

Ten minutes later, she stumbled back out into the cold, gasping for air, in need of another target, a realistic one, to keep her inevitable collapse at bay a little longer. She set off in search of the model village that both her children, but especially Phoenix, had loved so much, promising herself that there, where life was arranged to a manageable scale, she would be all right. But where was it? Had she taken a wrong turn? Was she confusing Weston with Minehead?

She sat down on a bench and looked out over the muddy beach to the distant islets of Steep Holm and Flat Holm, imagined she could hear the rise and fall of the distant tide and matched her breathing to it. She lay down, with Steep Holm at her feet and Flat Holm at her head, the wrong way up she thought, and forgot about breathing.

Then someone was tapping at her shoulder, and speaking to her in an old lady's shaky voice.

'Are you all right, my dear?'

'Bugger off. Let me die in peace.'

***

JJ STARED AT THE THREE WORDS THAT WERE written and over-written at the top of the otherwise blank page of foolscap in front of him: From the Doghouse. Perhaps a change of physical position might release the word-jam from his brain, like a thrombosis shoots suddenly towards the heart. His chair creaked as he stood. It didn't. He gave up.

In the garden, unpruned rose bushes stabbed at the February mist and the robin perched on the bird table reminding JJ of another missed milestone. He'd usually have cleared the crumbs from the breakfast table by now and put them out for the birds.

He shut the door of the Doghouse to keep in the heat and his slippered feet shuffled a trail through the stiff grass to the outside loo. Washing his hands, he caught sight of his reflection in the mirror above the basin. It was a sorry mess for certain, but no matter how hard he peered at himself he couldn't see what Katherine saw: a wrong and guilty man.

There was no towel. He walked back out into the garden, shaking his hands dry, and an idea flashed into his head. It must have been the shaking that did it. Twenty things to do with your extra time off during the three-day week. Obvious. Trivial. The kind of rubbish that would earn him a promotion.

He stood, equidistant from house and shed, and shook his hands harder in the hope of dislodging a better idea. The robin misunderstood and took flight, and it was their combined effort, man and nature working in harmony, which brought the final inspiration. He had knocked it out and was on the bus into town before Alan Watts had returned from lunch.

Watts was his usual non-committal self, twiddling his moustache as he glanced it over. 'Great,' was all he said, but then 'great' was all he ever said. Until today.

'But I don't get it,' he said.

'What don't you get?' said JJ, leaning forward over his copy, ready to explain.

'Well,' said Watts, his tone implying that what he was about to say was obvious to anyone but an idiot. 'You go on all year, week in week out, ranting on about politics, then as soon as they announce a general bleedin' erection you go off on a complete tangent. The only thing worth saying about this head case is that he should be locked up in the Ugandan equivalent of Barrow Hospital. Is his view of the most fragile political situation in this country since World War Two really more important than a general election? I'm not saying it's not good, John, it is good, but it's filler. Our readers rely on your strong opinions to help them form their own, John; you can't leave them high and dry at a time like this. I was about to commission you to deliver three columns a week for the duration of the campaign, one on each party per week, but I'm not interested in gossip and I'm worried now that you're not up to it. Are you up to it, John?'

After that morning's performance, JJ wasn't entirely sure he was, but this was a chance to influence the way people voted at the end of the month and he had to be up to it. Obviously Watts would edit out anything he deemed to be blatant partisanship in favour of JJ's beloved Labour party, but even so this was the opportunity he'd wanted all along without having realized he wanted it. And he'd be the only person to reverse a national trend and increase his workload from three days to full-time. He acknowledged that in his own dispassionate way his boss was trying to help him. 'Okay. I'll see what I can do,' he said. It didn't pay to show Alan Watts too much gratitude.

He knew that later, in the dim light of the Doghouse, his dwindling self-esteem would correct the fantasy, but for now, instead of sad old John Jacobs on the 365 bus to Long Ashton, he was Walter Kronkite aboard a jet to Vietnam, with a cigarette behind his ear and a hipflask in his pocket, and it was enough to fuel a hum of optimism.

He heard the rev of the Mini's engine as Katherine pulled up sharply behind the DS and the dull thud as her bumper hit his bumper followed by the ratchet pull of the handbrake. Door, footsteps, door. Only Katherine used the front door. Anyone watching the house from the bus stop across the road would assume she lived alone, although they'd have to be waiting for the bus bringing Godot to be there long enough to work it out.

He decided to stay out in the shed, to keep his head down and allow Katherine time to clock that he had cleared away the breakfast things, laid the fire, prepared dinner, time to add it all up and revise his position on the scoreboard in her head, that internal top ten, down which he had been tumbling in a terrible freefall.

He removed his gloves and rubbed his hands together, then spread his palms, fingers splayed Tommy Cooper-style, in the force field above the piles of paper that balanced, in no particular order, on his desk. Did Kronkite have to tidy up after himself? He went in for the tackle, slipping single sheets into files and folders, stapling longhand pages to typed ones, making new piles with anything that defied categorization. The rest he screwed up and threw in the bin.

A bang on the Doghouse door signalled Penny's homecoming. His habitual response was answered as usual by the slam of the back door. He zipped up his sleeping bag, rolled it into its own hood. He'd missed his afternoon nap, which accounted for the wave of exhaustion that for a moment weighed down his eyelids. But the real reason for his tiredness, the fact of having spent the night on a camp bed, unable to sleep at first for the cold, and then for the stink of the gas heater and the fear of going up in flames, were best forgotten. Because to remember last night was to remember that Katherine had said something truly dreadful to him, something worse than anything either of them had ever said to the other before - and they had said some pretty awful things in the course of their life together - something he could only hope and pray she was regretting after a night and day apart. It was time to go in.

As he stopped in the doorway for a second, watching her scrub potatoes in the sink, the cuffs of her sheepskin car coat, an ancient Christmas present from him to her, pushed up away from the dirty water, there were no obvious signs of the retraction he'd been wishing for, and then something snapped him awake. 'Stop!'

She kept going.

'What are you doing?'

'I'm washing potatoes for supper, what does it look like?'

This was good, the words were right. Wasn't this how they always spoke to each other? Almost. She looked up with contempt in her eyes but it was not, however, the usual contempt, the contempt of love.

'No, no, no,' he said, and rushed to the Aga. 'I've made tea. Shepherd's pie. In here.' He thrust out an arm as if in introduction: Aga, Katherine, Katherine, Aga. Now her shoulders would drop, her eyes soften and from that day on, shepherd's pie would be renamed humble pie, at least in JJ's recipe book. But he was running ahead of himself. Katherine *had* stopped what she was doing, *had* turned off the tap and *had* banged the potato down onto the draining board so that his lunchtime washing-up jumped and rattled with the shock. He'd made some ground and had to keep going. 'How was school?'

'Same as usual.'

'Where's Penny?'

'In her room.'

She was talking to him, they were having what might be called a conversation, but his sense of gaining ground had

74

an ominous undertow to it and he couldn't help feeling that by keeping going he would end up on his backside. So he shut up, and busied himself at the draining board, putting away the lunchtime dishes.

'Let's eat early then,' she said, as she left the room.

JJ listened to her slow heavy footsteps on the stairs.

He wandered into the sitting room to light the fire, and the fact of its already having been lit aggravated his sense of impotence. So he plonked himself down in the armchair, Katherine's armchair, marked by its crocheted cushion cover in purple, pink and orange, bought at the Gingerbread Christmas fair, where he had been Santa and everything was fine because then they had been a two-parent, two-child family in a comfortable enough position to reach out and offer support to the less fortunate one-parent families.

He had the urge to go and chat to Penny, to make small talk and get the gossip on the nuns, but only because it meant being upstairs and closer to Katherine. But it wouldn't be fair to sit in Penny's room, to encourage her to chatter away while he listened not to her but for evidence of sorrow from the room across the landing. No, he couldn't, but most of all because Katherine had pulled an invisible yet impenetrable screen across the bottom of the stairs and hung a notice on it saying: While I'm up here, you stay downstairs.

The first ever play they had seen together was *Who's Afraid of Virginia Woolf?* and it had provided the template for their future together. They had thought there was nothing that

75

could happen to them that couldn't be dealt with through confrontation; honest confrontation was where it was at, man. It was this awful non-confrontation that frightened JJ.

Through force of habit he switched on the TV for the evening news and caught the whining signature music at the end of *The Magic Roundabout*. The price of a loaf was up to fourteen-and-a-half pence, a half-pee off the political threshold, but he knew that already, there was nothing in the news that he hadn't already heard every hour on the hour on the Doghouse radio and read about in *The Guardian* after intercepting the paperboy at seven that morning, and in the *Post* when he'd gone into the office to deliver his copy. More fighting in Cambodia, Poulson sentenced to five years. But he watched anyway and suffered the daily five-minute Election '74 special afterwards as research for his new job. Why *hadn't* he dedicated his column to the election? Why hadn't it even occurred to him? No wonder the ends of Alan Watts's moustache had twitched when he'd read through his copy.

JJ stared into the fire. The flames blurred, logs gave off so much more smoke than coal. Perhaps the chimney needed sweeping. His thoughts were rescued by the sound of Penny, galloping down the stairs. JJ wiped his eyes on the sleeve of his writing jumper and his tears sat like tiny glass beads sewn into the oily fibres.

'Wedgie's been sick again,' said Penny as she charged past

the door. 'On my bed,' she said on her way back up again.

JJ raised a smile, not that anyone would see it, but it proved he could still do it. It was impossible to wallow with Penny around. Wedgie swaggered into the room having been given the heave-ho from Penny's bed and sat with his tabby back to the fire, his bullying gaze fixed on JJ's lap. JJ obliged by patting his knees, and Wedgie jumped up, turned three full circles and settled down with his backside rising and falling, following the pressure of JJ's stroking hand along the length of his spine.

When Penny had just started at St. Bernadette's and was having difficulty settling in - 'People keep staring at me, I'm a freak' - JJ had come home one day with two kittens from a litter born to the cat of one of his colleagues at the *Post*. 'You could at least call one of them Ted or Heath,' Katherine had said, 'for the sake of political balance.' But Penny had insisted, and Wedgie and Benn it was. 'They can smell a Tory a mile off,' JJ would say to Katherine. 'You feed them then,' Katherine would counter. She always voted Tory to torment him.

'Is that rubbish still on?' said Penny from the doorway.

He loved it when she mimicked his teasing. But whereas he would follow up by sidling in and standing in the centre of the room, pretending to watch with her as she sat twiddling her hair, watching one of 'her programmes', because in those relaxed moments she was his little girl again, Penny was content to deliver his opening line from the doorway and then saunter off into the kitchen in search

77

of something to pick at to spoil her appetite before tea.

JJ lifted his behind out of the chair, staying crouched in a sitting position so as not to disturb the cat, who was now curled up with his front paws covering his eyes as if he had fallen asleep halfway through a game of hide-and-seek. He turned down the volume on the television set and made it back to his seat with the cat undisturbed. 'Was it very bad?' he called out.

Penny reappeared. 'Was what very bad?'

'The vomit.'

'Oh no, it was more of a hairball.'

'Are you doing your homework?'

'I've done it.'

'Well, come and chat to your old dad then. How are the nuns?'

'Only if you switch that off.'

'You do it, love, I've just got up once and I don't think I'll get away with it a second time without disturbing the cat.'

Penny harrumphed over to the TV, with her head turned away from the screen and one hand clamped over her left ear, like an imbecile going in to defuse an IRA bomb. For a year she had been like that. She used to like watching the news, had even enjoyed the shared ritual of shouting at the television. JJ blamed her idiotic history teacher.

He watched her fold herself onto the sofa and cross one leg over the other, waving her top leg up and down like an oil derrick pumping in double time so that the platform shoe at the end of her swinging leg threatened to fly off and smash through the TV screen. JJ found himself ducking involuntarily each time it swung upwards. Something had annoyed her and she was itching to tell.

'Well, anything to report?' he said. 'Any new scientific discoveries surrounding the virgin birth that will save us from our imminent annihilation? And do you have to wear those shoes in the house? You're making me nervous. Where are your slippers?'

Penny clicked her tongue and rolled her eyes. 'Haven't you got anything new to say?' She nodded towards his chair. 'Mum's going to kill you.'

'I always sit here to watch the news.'

'Yeah, but you know she hates the cats sitting on her chair.'

'He's not on the chair, he's on me. Anyway, how come you're so keen to pick a fight today, fallen out with Jackwee?'

When Penny was thirteen, she had decided to sign her name 'Peni', in homage to her friend's adoption of the more exotic 'Jacqui'. The new signature had a spreading areola of an o above the i and by all accounts Sister Dementia had blushed when handing back Peni's biology homework. JJ had said 'Very Freudian, love' when she'd shown him but it had been her brother, Phoenix, with the vigilance of someone not without problems when it came to his own name, who pointed out, with relative patience, the obvious. JJ still liked to make oblique references to it by mispronouncing Jackie's name and Penny would blush like a Belisha beacon at the memory. This time, Penny groaned and slumped down onto the floor to crawl closer to the fire.

'You're blocking all the warmth,' she said in her complaining voice. 'Actually, Jackie's mum's got a new job.'

But JJ wasn't listening, he had heard a door shut upstairs and was listening to the sound of Katherine descending. Wedgie heard it too and leapt off JJ's lap to snuggle into a ball on the rug as if he'd been there all day.

JJ stretched his lips into a tense smile, but when Katherine appeared in the doorway she directed her words at Penny without even glancing at him. 'Penny, please come and set the table for tea.' There was a sharp edge to her voice that was nothing new when it came to her dealings with Penny and the notion flashed into JJ's mind that Katherine would probably have chosen to sacrifice her daughter if it had allowed her to save her son.

Penny turned to answer but Katherine had already disappeared and JJ sensed an objection about to erupt from his daughter.

'Go on love, I'm starving,' he said.

Penny tutted and struggled up onto her platforms. 'What're we having?'

'I've made a delicious shepherd's pie.'

'I think you should wait until we've tasted it before you use words like "delicious".'

The conversation over dinner, what precious little there was of it, was swinging his way, almost providing a convenient space for him to slot in the news of his temporary promotion at work. Then some trite comment escaped from Penny's mouth, which in itself was nothing out of the ordinary, and for a moment Katherine's response was to relax the hostile glare that had become her preferred facial expression in his company and replace it with a disbelieving gawp. At least she'd acknowledged his presence before throwing her cutlery across the table. Then she was out of her chair and up the stairs in a flash.

Of course he followed her, took her a hot-water bottle in the vain hope of thawing the ice that had amassed in the ever-widening chasm between them. But by then she had locked herself in the bathroom and refused to come out, leaving him with no choice but to go down to watch *Panorama* alone. There was no fun in it without her, no entertainment to be had from Harold Wilson's knowing jibe about Ted Heath's wanting to 'do it by the back door'. JJ had been ostracized, banished, with no option but to spend another night of discomfort and misery in the Doghouse. Sleeping in Phoenix's room was unthinkable and although he was nobbut a hack and well acquainted with the use of cliché, he could not bring himself to spend the night on the settee because it would upset Penny. A night spent in the Doghouse could at least be attributed to the pressures of his new job. It had to be acknowledged that the name he had given his shed was coming into its own.

He didn't dare examine Katherine's accusations in too much depth. What parent doesn't feel guilty at the death of a child, whatever the circumstances? Katherine was

81

deflecting her own sense of guilt onto him, that much he knew. He comforted himself by planning to pass the next few days making her life as easy as possible while keeping a low profile; he would leave her to work it out for herself. A few nights spent in the Doghouse would be a small price to pay to have her back, his playmate and sparring partner. He couldn't abide people who recalled the spirit of the Blitz at every minor drama, but in his days as a political journalist he had encountered many who had suffered so much worse.

And so he whistled as he made himself up a flask and a hot-water bottle, stuffed a couple of cushions under his arm and tried to be cheerful in his martyrdom. Perhaps he could use the time constructively, begin work on that novel he had always fancied himself writing.

He shoved the hot-water bottle into his sleeping bag, lit the heater and sat down at his desk with a fresh pad of foolscap, the top line of which he adorned with the title From The Doghouse. The same title as his column, but another might occur later.

Next to the heading he drew a little cartoon sketch of his shed, added a chimney to its roof and curtains to its lone window. A thin line of smoke coiled from the disproportionate chimney, as no smoke had ever done; smoke wasn't like that, stiff and unidirectional, it was like grief, it wove itself into the fabric of your life and before you realized it was there, it was already suffocating you.

He put down his pen; he had misjudged his mood. If he'd

struggled to find a subject worthy of five hundred words for a column in the local paper when the physical world around him was falling into ruin - Government Brought to its Knees by Industrial Action (by The People!), IRA Bombs Mainland Britain, School Building Scrapped, Racism Rife, England Fail to Qualify for World Cup for First Time in Footballing History, Oil Prices at Record High - and when the country was experiencing earth tremors, dense fogs, blackouts and freak gales, how could he possibly expect to rattle off an opus worthy of Fowles or Ballard overnight?

He switched off the light and the heater, zipped himself into his sleeping bag and, lulled by the rattle of a trapped moth striving towards some distant glimmer invisible to the human eye, he fell asleep.

He emerged stiff-backed from his hermitage at five and went into the house to do his morning chores. He roused Katherine and Penny from their sleep at the usual times. Katherine had slept in her coat.

Fancying himself as something of a flâneur, the best method JJ knew of clearing his head was to walk, a good wander over fields and through woods. He set off, planning to stay out until Katherine had left for work, to keep out of her way. He crossed over the road and walked past the Cider Institute and up the lane towards the psychiatric hospital. There was no traffic and no sign of human activity anywhere. He followed the winding lane over the railway bridge and as far as the orchard. He stared through the chainlink fence at the trees not yet in bud and forced himself to imagine the display of blossom that would come in just a few weeks. Phoenix and Penny had loved the orchard when they were small.

When he returned home the Mini was gone, and when he wiped his feet on the kitchen doormat Penny was shovelling cornflakes into her mouth, *The Guardian* and *Mirror* folded and untouched on the table in front of her.

'I fancied a walk,' he said. 'Would you like some toast?'

'Yes please.'

'Rare, medium or burnt to a cinder?'

'As if there's any choice. Can't we get a decent toaster?'

JJ cut two slices of bread and dropped them into the toaster. 'More tea?'

'No ta. It's stewed.'

JJ poured himself a cup. Stewed was how he liked it. 'Anything exciting happening at school today?'

'What do you think?'

Envying his daughter the oblivion of youth, JJ sat down at the table and unfolded the *Daily Mirror*: Petrol Fifty Pence a Gallon. Then *The Guardian*: Anonymous Capitalists Attempt to buy NUM out of Strike.

'DAD!'

JJ looked up. Penny, spoon in mouth, was jabbing a finger in the direction of the toaster, which was emitting a cloud of smoke and the stink of scorched bread. 'Sorry love,' he said. He got up and switched the toaster off at the plug and used a knife to dislodge the too-thick slices from their wire cages. 'It's not too bad. It's just the crusts. Do you want me to scrape it?'

'Oh, give it here or I'll miss the bus.' Penny held out a hand for her slice and sunk her teeth into it.

'Aren't you going to have anything on it?'

'Can't be bothered.'

'What about your teeth?'

'Ditto.'

When Penny had gone, he ran himself a bath in the hope that washing, shaving and discarding his smelly clothes for clean would wake him up. It worked to a degree: his head felt lighter under washed hair, his face more streamlined once rid of its itchy stubble, but he had been kidding himself if he'd imagined any improvement in the state of his personal hygiene would have any bearing on life in general.

And so he spent the day away from home, wandering over the fields at the back of the house and up into the woods beyond. When he returned home hours later he came through the gap in the back hedge and so failed to see the panda car parked in the drive.

Penny was already home, in the kitchen, making tea for three people. 'The bloody police are here again,' she said.

Without You

PENNY WOKE IN THE MIDDLE OF THE NIGHT. Her pillow was damp and sticky under her cheek. She'd dreamed that JJ had fallen asleep with the heater on and that the Doghouse had burned down. Her father had perished while she and Katherine looked on like two children waiting for baked potatoes on Bonfire Night, warming their hands in the heat of the flames. And all Katherine could say about it was 'Silly bugger', in the affectionate tone she reserved for JJ's regular acts of stupidity.

Penny pulled back the curtain and propped herself up on her elbow to look out. All was as it should be: no flames, no plumes of smoke lit silver by the moon, no moon at all, the Doghouse a solid shape in the blackness. Penny shivered, turned her pillow over, snuggled down and went back to sleep.

On the way to school her dream flashed into her mind once more, teasing itchy tears into the corners of her eyes. And when Jackie sat down next to her without a single word of greeting or otherwise, Penny had to swallow hard and stare at the finger-smeared window to avoid showing herself up by snivelling in public.

They travelled together in impeccable silence, right to the point of separation at the school entrance. They were still friends; it was just that neither of them knew what to say next. When they sat together as usual at lunch, and wandered arm in arm around the games fields afterwards, they were the same gum-chewing, sluttish gang of two they had always been, although, thought the nasty side of Penny's brain, only one of them really was a slut. The generous and good side of her brain grappled with an idea that sounded more like something from Cathy and Claire's problem page in *Jackie* than anything that made sense in real life: that Jackie losing her virginity in her best friend's house to her best friend's brother might have been nothing more than the most obvious, best and safest logical next step towards adulthood. Jackie couldn't have known Phoenix was about to die. And who knew how things might have turned out if he'd lived?

If she was honest, it had been obvious at Christmas that Phoenix fancied Jackie, even if the reverse attraction had come as a shock. He'd barged into her room on Boxing Day while she was sitting on her bed reading her Christmas issue of *Jackie*.

'So have you done it yet, our sprog?'

'Done what?' she'd said, in the special tired voice she had perfected for such conversations.

'You know, played hide the sausage, had reason to write to Cathy and Claire.'

'Is everyone at Oxford as stupid as you?'

'Don't play the innocent with me, missy. You've done it, haven't you? Who's the lucky boy then?'

'For god's sake, you're obsessed. And if this is your way of coming round to the subject of your own sordid little secrets, you can forget it now. I don't want to know. And if you've managed to get yourself a girlfriend at last don't bring her here because I won't be able to stop laughing.'

'Andandand,' Phoenix had said. 'Now now, Penguin, I'm just taking an interest in the well-being of a younger sibling. Obviously you can't confide in the parents so it's only right and proper that I should offer a friendly, more experienced ear.'

'Nothing to do with spreading gossip among your sex-starved morons for mates, then. Go away and mind your own business.'

'You are my business. You're my special sister. No need to be so touchy, it only makes me more convinced that you've got something to hide. Makes me suspicious that it might be someone I know. Who was it? I'll knock his block off.'

Phoenix had jumped into a boxer's pose and jigged on the spot in front of her as if waiting for the starting bell. Penny had continued to fiddle with the pages of *Jackie*, not reading or even looking at the pictures, just ignoring him and trying not to laugh. Then the record on her music centre outplayed her patience and she sat up to take it off, accidentally scratching the vinyl as the needle dragged across it.

'Tut tut,' said Phoenix. 'You can stack more than one record on there at once, you know.'

He was such a know-it-all. 'I thought you were going out.'

'I am indeed,' he said. 'But I thought I'd come in here to check up on the virginal status of my favourite sister before I ride off into the night.'

'How very thoughtful of you.'

'What are you doing tonight?'

'Jackie's coming round.'

'The lovely Jackie. She's done it loads of times. Written all over her. You Catholic schoolgirls are all the same.'

'You've got a one-track mind. And just because the school's Catholic, doesn't mean we have to act like nuns.' Penny sighed and reached across to switch on her transistor radio.

'What time's she coming?'

'Who?'

'Jackwee, idiot brain.'

'After you've gone out.'

'Shame. Is she staying over?'

'Why, what's it got to do with you?'

'That means she is.'

'Go AWAY.'

'You like this song. You love Simon Park. I saw your foot tapping when they were on Top of the Flops.'

'Piss. Off. Or I'll tell Mum you put cat's piss in Tim's coffee.'

(He had. Every Friday night of his last months at home,

Phoenix and his mates had spent the evening at the Rising Sun and then caught the bus into town to watch the late night X-rated film at the Odeon. A taxi ride afterwards brought them all back to the Jacobs house to smoke fags and lark about. One such Friday, they'd been to see The Exorcist and Phoenix and Rob were making coffee for everyone when Rob had discovered a puddle of cat's pee caught in the fold of a plastic bag on the kitchen floor and had spooned it into Tim's drink.

When Tim lifted his mug towards his mouth Phoenix and Rob collapsed into giggles. After a few sips Tim refused to drink more until they told him what was going on. When all had been revealed, Tim ran out of the house, shoved two fingers down his throat and vomited against the wall of the Doghouse.

Penny hadn't had the honour of witnessing any of this first-hand, but Phoenix had told her about it during one of their 'what's the worst thing you've ever done' confessionals.)

'Oh no, please don't tell Mummy and Daddy,' he'd said.

'You're wrong in the head,' said Penny.

'You're frigid.' And he left the room, mimicking Penny's flounce. He immediately reopened the door and put his head round. 'Tell Jackie I won't be late home if she wants to go ahead and warm the bed up.'

She had taken aim with her platform but he managed to slam the door shut a split second before it hit him in the face.

It seemed to Penny that in refusing to speak to each

other she and Jackie had stumbled naturally into the perfect interim solution to their problem. The only thing they could do was wait for a shared moment of either hilarity or mutual disgust or high drama to jolt them out of their shock and force them to resume their friendship naturally. That moment didn't happen that day at school, or on the bus home, but maybe it would the next day, or the day after that.

The Doghouse was in darkness when she got home, but Penny banged on the door anyway out of habit and out of a need to make noise, she'd been so quiet all day. There was no one in the house either. She was unbuttoning her coat on her way upstairs when someone knocked at the front door.

There were two of them, a man and a woman. Penny recognized them when they removed their hats as the same man and woman that had delivered the news about Phoenix.

'Is Mr Jacobs at home?' said the woman.

'No,' said Penny, wondering if it was illegal for her to be in the house on her own.

'When do you expect him home?'

She needed to get them off that subject, just in case. Her parents had always told Penny to think of the police as ordinary people doing a job, which was all very well when they were booking them for speeding, but a different matter when they kept turning up on the doorstep with bad news, because this was definitely bad news, she could tell by the way they only wanted to speak to JJ. The Jacobs family now had their own private bad news constables.

'Has something happened to Mum?'

'I'm afraid we have to wait and speak to your father,' said the woman. 'But your mother is fine and in good hands.'

In good hands. What was that supposed to mean? They made it sound like she needed to be held down, or sewn back together, but at least that meant she was alive.

Penny stared past the policewoman's shoulder. Over the road, a girl sat on the wall outside the Cider Institute. Penny saw her there every day after school in her navy blue uniform, the uniform the kids who went to the Comprehensive wore, waiting for the private bus that would take her up the lane to the mental hospital. Penny scanned the road from side to side, over the vision of the girl as if she were part of the wall and nothing more. Where was JJ?

'Would you mind if we came in to wait?'

Penny stepped to one side and held the door open for them, and showed them through to the sitting room, the least untidy option. They sat down, one at each end of the settee. Penny hoped they weren't expecting her to sit between them.

'I expect he'll be back soon,' she said. 'He's usually here when I get home. Shall I make some tea?'

'Thank you,' they said in unison.

She was about to carry the tea through to them when JJ appeared at the back door. At least he'd cleaned himself up. If you didn't look at his shoes, which were covered in mud, he looked almost presentable. Before he could start

94

with his usual questions about the nuns, Penny told him the police were there.

'What do they want?' he said. 'How long have they been here?'

'Calm down. Only a few minutes. How do I know what they want? No one tells me anything. They're in the sitting room. I've made tea. Do you want this other one?'

'Thanks love, I'll take them through. I think you should come too.'

'No thank you, not on your life. They said mum's in good hands, whatever that means. Take your shoes off.'

He didn't hear or else he ignored her. Penny sat down at the kitchen table and flicked over the pages of the *Daily Mirror*, or what was left of it after JJ had taken his clippings, half-listening to the murmur of voices from behind the sitting room door. It was like hearing the TV news coming up through the floor of her bedroom; she was intrigued by what might be being said, but also didn't want to know.

After ten minutes or so her dad reappeared, trailed by the two constables, a blank expression on his face. Penny stood to attention at once.

'Your mum's all right, love,' he said. 'But she's in Weston General. They're keeping her in overnight for observation, so I expect we'll be able to bring her home tomorrow.'

'What's wrong with her, has she been in a car crash?'

'No,' said JJ. 'I don't really know what happened. I'll ring the hospital shortly. They think she's suffering from exhaustion.'

'Exhaustion? Why, what's she been doing?' Penny was confused. Wasn't exhaustion associated with physical overexertion? There'd been no evidence of that lately where Katherine was concerned; she'd had been in bed before the nine o'clock news every night for weeks.

'There are lots of reasons why people get worn out, love. It isn't always related to anything they've been doing.'

Penny was about to tell him he was talking gibberish when the policeman cleared his throat and thrust his piggy face - Phoenix used to call them pigs - forward to speak.

'We'll be getting on now, sir. If you'd like, we could give you a lift to Mrs Jacobs's car?'

'That's very kind of you, but I may as well pick it up tomorrow on the way to the hospital. Oh, well, assuming it'll be all right where it is?'

'Oh yes, it's fine. The local chaps locked it up and we'll get them to keep an eye on it overnight for you.'

JJ thanked them and showed them out. Penny waited until he'd finished shepherding them through the front door, then went to join him in the hall. He was standing next to the telephone table clutching a page torn from the police officer's notebook and pulling at the hair at the back of his neck.

'Are you going to call them now?' she said.

'Yes. Pour us another tea, love.'

'Please.'

Feeling braver now, she strained to hear his side of the conversation over the rising ssshh of the kettle, but he had lowered his voice. When he came into the kitchen he sat down and rested his elbows on the table, still holding the piece of paper. His head bowed forwards to rest against his hands, but stopped midway, as if he had run out of energy before the action could be completed.

'Did you speak to her?'

'No, they've transferred her. She's up at Barrow.'

'What? The loony bin, what's she doing there?' Penny wanted him to say they'd sent her there because it was closer to home, but it was pretty clear he was going to say no such thing.

'I don't know exactly, love, I'll find out tomorrow. I've made an appointment to see the doctor there. I expect she needs a good rest.'

'A rest? She can rest here, why does she have to go there to do that?'

JJ looked at her as if he was about to embark on one of his long explanations, but then he sighed and looked down at the piece of paper in his hand, as if he knew exactly why she was there, but either couldn't be bothered to tell her, or had guessed - rightly - that Penny's question was rhetorical, that she didn't really want the nitty-gritty of it, that she was angry at her mother for drawing yet more attention to their household.

'That's what I'll find out tomorrow,' he said. 'I expect they'll keep her in for a couple of days to check she's okay, and then she'll come home to be looked after. Did you make that tea? I need to go and phone David Browning before he goes home.'

'And tell him what? There's only one more day 'till half term. Can't you just leave it or say she's got the 'flu?'

'She didn't turn up at work today so he has to know, love, he's her boss. I won't be specific, I'll tell him she's not well. I don't know any more than that myself.'

Penny poured the tea. Her mum had gone mental and her dad was behaving as if she had nothing worse than a mild stomach ache. Thank god she and Jackie weren't speaking, at least she'd be spared the embarrassment of telling her that her mother was a nutter. She passed him his cup, slopping brown liquid over the rim and into the saucer. He took it, tipped the spillage back into the cup without saying anything, and rose from his seat.

'Thanks love, have you got homework to do?'

'Bloody Nora, you can't expect me to go to school tomorrow, surely.' Penny directed a sneer of disbelief in her father's direction and stomped out of the room and up the stairs and slammed the door of her bedroom behind her to shut out the whirr of the telephone's dial and her dad's muffled tones.

When Phoenix died Penny had followed her parents' suit, cried when they cried, carried on as normal when they did; she had taken her cues from them, because she had been stupid enough to think they knew best how to deal with the situation. But now they were each of them trying to out-mad the other, what the bloody hell was she supposed to do?

***

TWO DAYS LATER, Penny received a letter in the post. She recognized the writing on the envelope, in fact she'd spent most of third year at school trying to copy its rounded letters and circular full stops and i-dots in her own handwriting. Jackie had sent it first-class and written URGENT on the back flap of the envelope. Penny ripped open the envelope and took it up to her room.

> *Right Our Pen,*
> *I hope you are well. I was right worried when you didn't come to school today. I'm writing to you because my Mum and Dad are going to book a holiday in Spain for the Easter holidays and said if you would like to you can come with us. If you want to come (I hope you do coz Marc and Dave might be there!!!!!!!) ask you're parents and let me know after half term. It will cost about £50 plus spending money. I'm staying with my Nan for half term (yawn). See you next week.*
> *Lots of love*
> *Jacqui*

Penny read the letter again in case she had misunderstood. Spain! No, hang on: SPAIN!!!! Maybe Marc and Dave would be there; it was the kind of place pop stars would go. Better still, Jackie wanted her to go, and that meant they were still best friends. Their holiday plans would give them something to talk about when they went back to school after half term, and hopefully right up to Easter. But, fifty pounds! She had ten quid in pound notes that she'd saved from her Saturday job and stashed in the cigar box in her room where Phoenix couldn't find it. She ran downstairs to check the calendar in the kitchen.

The Easter holidays began on March thirtieth so she had roughly six weeks to save another forty pounds. Maybe Barker's would let her work more over half term to earn extra money. Even if they didn't, there was time to save the rest from her Saturday money, as long as Jackie's parents didn't want the money before the holiday, and as long as she didn't buy anything else in the meantime.

JJ would object to her going on the grounds of Spain being a fascist dictatorship hellhole blah blah bloody blah, so she decided not to tell him just yet and to say yes on her parents' behalf as they'd both disappeared anyway. She would tell either one or both of them later when things had settled down a bit. And by then it'd be too late to stop her going.

As JJ didn't come in to make her breakfast, Penny got dressed and went out without eating, leaving a note on the kitchen table to tell him she'd gone into town. The note was still there when she came home three hours later with a Horizon holiday brochure rolled up under her arm.

Despite there being no one to hide it from she kept it hidden as she ran up the stairs, as she had seen Phoenix do hundreds of times with copies of magazines him and his filthy mates passed around.

The first 'o' in Horizon was drawn as a big yellow sun, under which a smiling sun-soaked family waved tanned arms at her from the edge of a pool. She drooled over the glamorous resort names: Benidorm, Torremolinos, Lloret de Mar, Malaga. Each destination had its own temperature chart: seventy-two degrees in April. Hotter than summer!

'*Stackridge?*' said Penny, pretending to choke on her chips. JJ had insisted on her eating dinner in the Doghouse with him because he had a surprise for her, and she'd gone along with it to cheer him up even though she knew his surprises and they were never up to much. Even so, she hadn't imagined it would be quite as disappointing as tickets for a Stackridge concert. He'd obviously misinterpreted the spirit in which she'd agreed to go to the Carpenters concert if Katherine wasn't home next week. She'd only said yes thinking that Katherine would definitely be home to let her off the hook. She would have felt sorry for him having to miss out on seeing his favourite singer, but not so sorry that she wanted to make a habit of going to concerts with him. 'What, "Purple Spaceships over Yatton" Stackridge?'

JJ was so chuffed with himself his head was moving up and down like a nodding dog. He'd seen it advertised in the *Evening Post*. It was in a couple of weeks' time and he'd bought three tickets, so even if Katherine was home there was no getting out of it.

'I thought we could go in honour of Phoenix,' he'd said. 'A sort of pilgrimage.'

'Dad. The only good thing about Phoenix not being around is that we don't have to listen to that rubbish any more. All his mates will be there, they'll see us.' What she meant was that they would see him, and see the state he was in, but she couldn't bring herself to say it: he was looking dejected enough already.

'What's wrong with that? Wouldn't it be nice to see them all again? It's been too quiet around here lately; perhaps they could come back with us after the show.'

'What and all cram out here in the shed? Look, Dad, it's not as if Phoenix has never seen Stackridge, he's seen them loads of times, and he wouldn't be going to this one anyway, he'd have been in Oxford. Get Mum to go with you if you're so keen on it.'

'She may not be home by then.'

'Why, how long is she going to be up there? She can't be that bad.'

'I don't know how long she'll be there. The doctor said maybe a month. And that's the other thing I wanted to tell you, the doctor would like to see us both on Monday afternoon.'

'Who, you and me?' Already Penny's plans to work and earn money towards her holiday were under threat.

'Why does he need to see me as well? I'm all right. It's only Mum that's gone mad, well, and you, but there's nothing wrong with me.'

'Who,' said JJ. '*Who's* gone mad. Nobody said there was anything wrong with you, love, and I'm fine. I'm sure Mum will be too. I think he just wants to make sure that we all know what's going on so we can all help her to get better.'

'So have they worked out what's wrong with her?'

'She's just a bit depressed, that's all, and needs some rest.'

'Depressed? I get depressed all the time, you don't see me marching up to the loony bin and demanding a bed. Why can't she be depressed here like the rest of us?'

'Why don't you ask the doctor on Monday? He can answer your questions better than I can. I don't know much more than you do, love.'

It was a complete fob off, but Penny's fish and chips were getting cold, so she shut up and ate, staring into the solid orange face of the Calor gas heater. Between mouthfuls she summoned up one last sarcastic gem. 'Great surprise, Dad. Smart. I thought you were going to make an announcement about something drastic like you planning to shave off your beard.'

'Ah well, now you come to mention it, look what else I got today.' He rummaged around under his chair and pulled out what looked like an oversized glasses case. He held it out towards her and flipped it open. Penny had seen advertisements on television for such gadgets; they

103

were used by men with already close-shaven faces, not men with Hampton Court Maze on their mush.

'Big deal,' she said. 'That'll never get through the foliage on your face. Watch out for birds' nests.'

'I'll trim it first,' he said.

They ate in silence a while longer.

'Can we go in the car?'

'Where, to Stackridge?'

'On Monday, to the hospital.' Penny knew what was coming next. Why did she even bother trying to get her family to be normal?

'I thought we could catch the hospital bus. It stops outside the Cider Institute at four fifteen and there's one coming back at six. It's free so we may as well use it and save petrol. Either that or walk.'

She groaned. At least it was half term and that girl wouldn't be there. She'd just have to pray that no one she knew would see her getting on or off the bus. Pray for thick smog. 'Okay then, Dad,' she said. 'If I've got to come on the nutters' bus with you, then you've got to promise to do something about the state of this place because it's really starting to reek.'

The combined effects of shed-smell, Calor gas fumes and fish supper were inadequate to neutralize the stink of stale body odour that pervaded the air in the Doghouse and now that she had finished eating Penny was itching to get away from it and back to her holiday brochure. She screwed her fish and chip wrapper into a ball in such a hurry that she forgot to remove the fish leftovers for Wedgie and Benn.

'What about Stackridge? If I tidy up will you come with me?'

'We can talk about it when you've done it,' she said. 'Right, I'm going in.'

'Catch,' said JJ, and threw his newspaper ball at her. It bounced off her shoulder.

'That could have hit the heater and caught fire,' she said. 'Am I the only one round here with any common sense?'

Before dumping the wrappers in the dustbin, Penny walked around the side of the shed and knocked on the window. With her index finger she rubbed a backwards B.O. in the thin film of dirt that covered the glass pane.

Sitting in Katherine's favourite chair with her legs stretched out across the pouffe, and *Hawaii Five-O* on the telly, Penny flicked through her brochure for the millionth time that day: palm trees, blue sky, golden sand, judging by the photos Spain was probably not all that different to Hawaii. She had been to the south of France, but she didn't want it to be like that, she wanted it to be more glamorous and less smelly. All the boys would look like Marc and Dave and there'd be no other girls there so she and Jackie would have first dibs. Their hotel rooms would be spotless; in fact they'd be so brand spanking new that they would be the first people to sleep in the beds. Pioneers. Penny looked around at the sitting room with its ancient and sagging furniture, marked with cat scratches and cup

105

rings. What a dump. Not much better than the Doghouse, only without the smell. For instance, when had the curtains last been washed, if ever? Now she had the house to herself she could make whatever improvements she wanted. There were three windows in the sitting room, six curtains.

Removing the curtain hooks from the eyes under the pelmet was fiddly and made her arms ache but being tall had some advantages, netball not being one of them. Everyone at school expected her to be good at netball, but she hated the bloody game; to catch the ball and then stop with it went against every natural instinct. She removed all the hooks which had probably once been white but which neglect had turned grey and dropped them into a bowl of hot soapy water to soak. She stuffed the curtains into the washing machine.

The tops of the pelmets were thick with dust. Penny filled a bucket with hot water, shook some scouring powder into it and threw in the dishcloth. One wipe across the top and the cloth was coated with a solid layer of black grime. She squeezed it out into the bucket and repeated the process until she had cleaned all three and the water was the colour of a miner's bath. As she carried the bucket to the kitchen sink the rocking water revealed a greasy black tidemark clinging to its sides.

She found a rusting spray can of furniture polish and a duster at the back of the cupboard under the sink and started on the sideboard. She felt like one of those women

106

in the television adverts, glamorous like Jackie's mum. If only she had a flowerdy housecoat.

By midnight the sitting room was transformed into as close an approximation of a spotless modern home as a rambling Georgian cottage stuffed with every style of furniture made since the Industrial Revolution could.

Her hands were rough, their skin dried out by hot water and scouring powder, but as JJ had ruined her plans to work on Monday, she pledged to use that time to tackle the rest of the house. She had to get up for work the next morning, and that day at work would earn her a good long lie-in on Sunday and bring her a little bit closer to Spain.

***

JJ ARRIVED FOR HIS FIRST APPOINTMENT AT THE hospital optimistic that Katherine would be coming home with him afterwards. He left a short while later with the impression of having sealed a contract that he'd had no part in drafting.

A familiarity in Dr O'Grady's manner had put JJ at his ease from the start, and he was impressed by the way the doctor flicked out the vent of his jacket like a pianist as he sat down; the action implied an assuredness in his own accomplishment, as if Katherine's problem was no more than a composition that had been incorrectly notated and simply required the hand-eye coordination of an expert to tweak it back to perfection.

'How many children have you, Mr Jacobs?'

'One. Now. A daughter. We lost our son, our eldest, last month in a motor bike accident.' JJ stopped speaking, horrified that tears were collecting in the well of his eyelids: was it already so long since Phoenix had died?

'I am sorry to hear that, John. However, it does help my understanding of the situation a little. When I asked your, er, Katherine that same question she changed her first answer of two to one and then explained her indecision by saying that you had made one of the children up in some kind of game.'

JJ shook his head, the best response he could muster. He was contemplating a stain at the hem of his trousers from petrol spillage when he'd fetched Katherine's Mini and the nozzle of the petrol can had been damned tricky to fit into the car's tank.

'Grief is a very difficult and complicated emotion to deal with, John. How are things at home, with your daughter and yourself?'

JJ swallowed hard. If he weren't careful, this man would have him blubbing like an infant. 'We're okay I suppose. Penny seems to be coping. When can I see Katherine?'

'She was extremely tired when she arrived, so I have her under sedation just now. When she wakes up I'll have another chat with her and her supervising nurse before I make a full diagnosis. Why don't you give me a call tomorrow afternoon and we'll get you back in for a longer chat with me or one of my colleagues. Do you have anything else you would like to ask me?'

'No. Well, yes. How long will she be here?'

'That I cannot say as yet. It may be possible to give you a better idea of what to expect tomorrow. Is that all right?'

JJ nodded and they both stood.

The doctor extended a hand. 'Thank you for coming in, and please be assured that Katherine will receive the best of care here. And please feel free to call at any time if you need to. If I am not available then one of my team will be able to help you.'

JJ took his hand and shook it. Then something else occurred to him. 'Do I need to sign anything?'

'Oh no,' said the doctor. 'Katherine is here voluntarily.'

'I see. Thank you. I'll call tomorrow then. We're only down the road you know, so it'll be no problem coming in to visit.' JJ was unsure whether her being there voluntarily was a cause for optimism or alarm.

'Yes, that'll be very advantageous at the appropriate time. Goodbye, John. Let me show you out.' He led JJ down a corridor the colour and smell of yesterday's cabbage. They shook hands again at the door and the doctor walked back towards his office.

Somewhere in the woods beyond the edge of the car park a blackbird trilled its nonsensical song, predicting the end of winter, reminding JJ he wasn't ready for spring.

The next morning at seven he walked to the phone box in the village to call the hospital, but he was too early. The night nurse was about to go off duty and explained in a tired voice that Katherine had slept well and was not awake yet. She assured him if he called again after two o'clock the doctor would have had the opportunity to review Katherine's assessment. In the meantime, she suggested, he might like to pack a few essentials for Katherine and bring them to his next meeting with the doctor. Which is how JJ came to be sitting at the kitchen table twiddling a biro between thumb and index finger and staring at a sheet of paper.

He'd been there for half an hour when Penny came down in her dressing gown in search of the cup of tea he would normally have taken up to her. She seemed surprised to see him there.

'Why are you writing in here, can't you stand the smell out there any more?'

'There's no need to be rude. I'm making a list of things to take to your mum.'

Penny moved closer and looked at the paper. It was blank but for the letter K in its top right-hand corner, written and overwritten so many times that the ink was smudged.

'I thought you said she was coming home.'

'She will be, but they asked me to bring her a few essentials.'

'That's not much of a list. She'll need more than that.'

JJ put his pen down. 'I can't think of anything.'

Penny went and filled the kettle. 'Knickers,' she said.

'What?'

'Knickers, write it down. And tights, and bras. Underwear. You know, the things people wear under their clothes, *and change every day.*'

JJ ignored the sarcasm and wrote the words, relieved to be told what to do.

'Has she got a nightie?'

If Katherine wore anything in bed she slept in her bra and knickers, like a movie star, and in the transition period between sleeping and dressing she covered herself with JJ's threadbare dressing gown: she didn't possess one of her own. 'I don't think so, she can have my pyjamas.'

'That's no good. She'll have to have a nightie in hospital. And a new dressing gown. We'll have to go into town and buy her one. Marks and Sparks or British Home Stores. There'll probably be other stuff she needs anyway.'

This was going to be expensive, but it would be worth every penny if it brought Katherine home sooner. Penny spoke as if it was a statistically proven fact that patients with new nightwear were discharged more quickly from hospital than those in their old gear, or their husband's pyjamas. While he doubted its logic, he was prepared to go along with it; there was no accounting for the psychological impact of new things, that very notion had been singlehandedly responsible for a new world order, so who was he to argue. With that in mind he added the silk blouse he had given Katherine for Christmas to the list. She'd refused to wear it to their New Year's Eve party in case she spilled wine on it and he'd suspected she didn't like it, but it was the last thing he had given her and it was new.

'Books,' said Penny.

Why hadn't he thought of that? 'Of course, her favourite plays, stuff she's read a million times before. Well done.'

By the time they completed the list it was still only seven-thirty. Penny refused to catch the same bus she usually caught to school so JJ fetched a suitcase from upstairs and opened it on the kitchen table. He had Penny run up and down the stairs to do the gathering while he folded and packed each item.

'Don't forget the blouse,' JJ bawled from the kitchen after Penny had failed to bring it for the third time. What was wrong with the blouse?

'All right, keep your hair on.'

In the end, JJ was grateful for their shopping trip and its petty arguments in Marks and Spencer over which style of nightdress would best suit Katherine's needs. It shortened the chasm between morning and afternoon and the time when he could call the hospital again.

He arrived at the hospital at ten to four. Before pulling the suitcase from the backseat of the Mini, he flipped open its lid and tucked a brown envelope under the elastic straps that held the contents of the case in place, on top of the family photograph the doctor's secretary had suggested including. Inside the envelope was a note, its message brief: *Come home soon, I can't fight alone.*

He wished he hadn't added the bit about fighting, he wasn't even sure what he meant by it, and it crowded the sentiment of the message by being over-dramatic. Had he meant it to be funny? However inappropriate, in whatever way, it was too late to change it and a botched message was better than no message at all. In a few days it would be Valentine's Day and in the whole of their twenty years together they had never been apart on that day, but he had stopped short of writing an early card; instinct told him it was too soon, in more ways than the obvious one.

'Mr Jacobs?' Someone touched his upper arm and JJ looked up at a smiling woman with yellow hair that looked as if it had been scraped out of a candyfloss machine, sculpted into blonde twirls and held together by a visible mist.

'Dr Wild is free now. Would you like more tea?'

The tea she had given him on arrival, along with the news that he would be meeting a different doctor today, had gone cold; if he refused another it might imply the first had been undrinkable, but he was too tired to worry about causing offence. 'No thank you, I'm fine.'

He followed her clicking heels across the parquet floor that led to Dr Wild's office, where book-lined walls and soft carpeting offered a blast of warmth after the institutionalized chill of the corridor.

The doctor rose to shake hands. 'Thank you for coming.'

'Thank you for seeing me. How's Katherine?'

'Please take a seat, Mr Jacobs.' He gestured towards two worn leather armchairs. JJ sat in one and the doctor took the other before continuing. 'You're seeing me because Katherine will be moving to a ward under my care later today. I have yet to meet her but I have read the Admissions consultant's report and he is satisfied that Katherine is in no danger of causing harm either to herself or to another person. However, she is unwell and has expressed a wish to remain here at Barrow for treatment until such time as we all agree she is ready to go home. She is suffering from reactive depression with anxiety, triggered by the grief resulting from the death of your son.' He paused. JJ nodded.

'Her anxiety presents in such a way that she is confused as to the proper circumstances of your son's death, and while hers is an extreme form of grief, it is by no means an unusual one. This is a time of crisis for you all and Katherine needs some additional support from outside the family to help her through it.'

The doctor blinked at JJ as if to signal the end of his diagnosis.

JJ realized he was expected to speak and shifted in his chair. 'What treatment will she be given?'

'For the time being she is taking diazepam for her anxiety, and amitriptyline, an antidepressant.'

'Mother's little helpers,' said JJ. He loved the Rolling Stones.

Dr Wild's smile somehow swerved clear of being

patronising. 'I understand your concerns, Mr Jacobs. May I call you John?'

Not wishing to interrupt, JJ nodded his consent.

The doctor continued. 'I carefully monitor the dispensation of all drugs, and I can assure you Katherine will be prescribed diazepam only for the duration of her stay in this hospital. Depending on how long that stay is, however, she may need to continue to take antidepressants for a while after being discharged. My aim is to have her home again within a month, but it may be a little longer depending on my team's assessment of her progress and needs. I can write this all down for you, if you like?'

The doctor turned to reach for a pad on his desk and, fearing the meeting was drawing to a close, JJ asked the only question he really wanted the answer to. 'When can I see her?'

'I'm afraid that is not for me to decide. An unfortunate symptom of her grief is that she holds you responsible for the death of your son. Is this something you are aware of?'

JJ nodded again, and turned to fix his gaze elsewhere, beyond the darkened window and his own head's ghastly reflection, which seemed to be floating disembodied, like a lost balloon, among the invisible trees beyond.

'How are you coping with your own grief, John?'

The doctor's voice was soothing. Too soothing. JJ shifted his focus to a single glass pane, in which his eyes were reflected as two black hollows. Those two black hollows were watering, from the effort of concentration, he told himself. The same effort of concentration that prevented him from speaking.

'I will in any case be writing to your GP to inform him of Katherine's admission here, and I will mention to him that you may also require some help from him.'

As JJ shook his head, two little reservoirs of tears overflowed into his bushy sideburns.

'Even in so-called normal circumstances grief can be very overwhelming, John. Katherine will be looked after very well here and I would advise you to take this opportunity to look after yourself. I believe you also have a teenage daughter. Is she close to her mother?'

'Fairly.' JJ's voice cracked, and he coughed it clear. 'Fairly. She's probably closer to me. Katherine was closer to Phoenix. Will Katherine be locked up while she's here?'

'No, no, not at all. It is normal procedure to admit all new patients onto a locked ward for close observation and initial assessment purposes, but that only lasts a day or two. After diagnosis we make a verbal contract with all our patients, with the exception of those who are extremely poorly, that they stay within the grounds and adhere to meal times and an eight o'clock curfew in the evening. Maybe you have noticed that the hospital gates are always open. We have two hundred acres of beautiful grounds here, some of the most ancient deciduous woodland in the whole of Europe. I'm sure you would agree it would be sacrilegious for us to deny the advantage of such surroundings to our patients. Only the most acutely ill are cared for on locked wards, mainly for their own safety. There is plenty to occupy patients at Barrow and Katherine will be encouraged to participate in as many activities as she can cope with. My ward is a community in its own right and a very welcoming one. And we are fortunate to have an excellent chef, so I eat on the ward myself as often as possible.'

JJ didn't doubt anything the doctor said, but the idea of total separation from Katherine scared him; he was to have no access to her, no insight into her changing thoughts and moods; it was as if she had died too.

'I have one more question for you, John, and then if there is anything else you would like to ask me, I would be happy to answer.' He paused for breath. 'Has Katherine suffered from depression at any other time in her life that you are aware of? After childbirth, perhaps?'

JJ was forced to allow his thoughts to revisit the place and time of his son's birth, where still more guilt was lodged. Katherine had been twenty, JJ twenty-one, and both midway through their second year at Oxford when Katherine became pregnant. JJ had taken a summer job at the *Gazette*, reporting about cats up chimneys to supplement their grant money, and they had survived. Phoenix was born towards the end of the summer holiday and they had flourished; they'd always been a sociable couple and were determined to continue as such and,

117

as the only parents among their peers, they were never wanting for a friend to give Katherine a hand while he was out working, or to babysit if they wanted a night out.

But motherhood proved more difficult to disguise than early pregnancy had been and when they returned for Michaelmas term of their final year Katherine was sent down for being an unmarried mother.

JJ had begged her to marry him, had even offered to leave too in solidarity, but she had been adamant they stick to their principles; she even refused to pretend they were married. A petition was got up at the university, but no new precedent was set and so he had stayed on and Katherine stayed home with Phoenix.

She had trained as a teacher when Phoenix started school - saying it was probably what she would have done anyway - and took her first job soon after Penny was born. JJ had his job for the *Post* by then and looked after Penny during the day, working when Katherine came home. JJ shook his head. JJ shook his head.

'Mmhmm,' the doctor nodded, as though he had been able to eavesdrop on JJ's thoughts. 'I see.' He put his notebook back on his desk. 'You look tired, John, you should go home to your daughter and rest. Why don't you call me tomorrow about this time, when I will have spoken to Katherine? It would be helpful if I could see you again after the weekend, and perhaps your daughter would like to come too?' He stood. 'Thank you again for coming in.

Is that Katherine's suitcase? I will have it taken to the ward.'

JJ reluctantly handed him the case, knowing it was pointless to ask if he could deliver it himself. 'Thank you, doctor,' he said.

He sat in the Mini. It was half past five and he was at the epicentre of the maelstrom of people leaving work, people coming on duty, people in suits, people in overalls, rushing to and from the car park, waving greetings and farewells. It was like watching a whole day pass at high speed - a day with no fluent narrative that jumped randomly back and forth - until at last all the cars surrounding his had gone and time slowed to its normal pace.

Any one of those people driving off might have seen Katherine, spoken to her, and he would know nothing of it. He was as removed from her life, as irrelevant, as he had been before they'd met. The event that had sealed their union, the birth of their son, was the seed of that which had as easily and swiftly wrenched them apart. JJ was reeling from two unexpected deaths, the second being the sudden death of his marriage, because that is what it was, a marriage; a church ceremony does not a marriage make, had been their answer to anyone who dared question their choice to remain unhitched. A child, however, had a marriage made, and the death of that child had broken it.

JJ slumped down over the steering wheel and dredged up the first real tears of his adult life. Not the happy tears, the kind that never quite brim over, at the birth of a child or the regulation quota at the funeral of a distant aunt, but real droplets dredged up from the well of his body, that splashed onto his thighs and left him gasping, exhausted and frozen.

At last he roused himself, turned the key in the ignition and turned the heater to full. Checking the rear view mirror before reversing he noticed that the steering wheel had left an imprint in his forehead like the scar of a clumsy lobotomy. He began the slow, short drive home, passing through the gates that were always open, that divided Katherine's world from his own.

It didn't help to know that those gates were always open, that the ward she was on was unlocked, that she could walk home in less than half an hour any time she liked, because she chose not to; she would rather be in that place than at home, with him. No, that didn't help at all. What might help, just a little, was for him to also make a decision that would realign their lives while they were apart. Until Katherine came back, he would not set one foot inside their house. He would go on strike, as they all had in their own way; even Penny had refused to go to school. In a strange solidarity with Phoenix all their lives had been postponed, not cancelled like Phoenix's had been, but put on hold until such time as they could be properly resumed.

JJ measured the parameters of his planned exile with some trepidation. The few domestic habits that could be incorporated into his Doghouse routine, combined with

120

his increased workload, would still provide insufficient activity to fill a whole day. In the absence of plot, characters and inspiration he'd already given up on his novel; resigned himself to the fact that his muse had forsaken him for someone more talented. He had tripped through life under the illusion that all experience is sufficient raw material from which a novel might be forged whenever the urge might summon him to pick up his biro, but the reality was dawning finally that not everyone is blessed with the skill to mould and transform that stuff into a work of art, be it painting, sculpture, play, film, novel or poem. Fiction is transformation, he concluded, journalism is writing. He was a journalist. And, given the difficulty he was having in transforming hard facts from the outside world into the required five hundred coherent words for a thrice-weekly column, he conceded it likely that even his journalistic badge was delusory.

On Monday morning he caught the bus into town, with the primary purpose of delivering his first column of the week but also with the intention of requesting a month's leave, to start immediately. Admittedly he was on dodgy ground having just agreed to increase his workload; he'd claim he needed the time for a special project, the details of which could not be divulged. But during the course of his chat with his editor, conducted with Watts lounging back in his swivel chair, silk-socked feet on desk, while

JJ slouched against the wall, two unexpected things happened. Unexpected thing number one was that JJ came right out and told him that Katherine had been admitted to Barrow. The second, even more remarkable given the gravity of the information he had just received, was that Watts refused point blank to allow him the time off, while at the same time pulling off a reasonable impersonation of a sympathetic human being.

'I'm sorry to hear that, John, really sorry to hear that,' he said. 'If there's anything else I can do to help, you know you only have to ask, but you can't desert us now, we need you here until the election is over. If you can give me that then I'll pay for you and Katherine to have a holiday, anywhere you like for as long as you want, when she comes home.' He swivelled to look up at JJ and started dramatically as if he'd noticed something shocking about him for the first time. 'Jesus, John, what's happened to your face? Or maybe I should say, what's happened to your face, Jesus? Here, let me show you something.' He lowered his feet and flicked through the early edition of the *Post* on his desk. 'Here,' he said, tapping a finger on an advertisement. 'Here you are, look. Boots battery shaver, three pounds twenty. Treat yourself. It's hard enough for the old folks these days without being confronted by a werewolf coming at them out of the smog.' Watts laughed at his own joke, the sound of a car driving too fast over a cattle grid, and changed the subject.

Either Alan Watts was a bigger bastard than JJ had

given him credit for, or his way of dealing with a crisis was to blast it with testosterone and see what happens; the man's way. JJ suspected the former.

Dr Wild ushered them into his office. A third chair had been placed alongside the one occupied by JJ at his previous appointment. 'You must be Penny,' he said, holding out his hand. 'Thank you for coming. Goodness, you look like your mother.'

To JJ's surprise, Penny shook his hand and thanked him, apparently without sarcasm, and he realized how rarely he got to observe his daughter interacting with strangers and felt a rush of gratitude for her composure and good manners.

The doctor explained that he had consulted with his staff and with Katherine, and that she seemed to be adjusting well to her treatment and to life in her new environment. She wasn't quite ready yet for a visit from JJ, but had agreed at some unspecified time in the future to attend an interview with the doctor with JJ present. He expressed a hope that this was acceptable to JJ, as he was inclined to consider this a significant step forward. Katherine had, however, shown considerable interest in a visit from Penny.

JJ noted Penny's reluctance to be pinned down to a date during half term, but eventually they agreed upon a time the following Tuesday after school. Katherine would meet her from the bus at four thirty, but if for any reason she was not there, the doctor suggested that, after their chat, they might walk past the ward so that Penny would know where to find her.

JJ jolted himself out of his sense of redundancy to ask: 'Is it safe for Penny to walk around here alone?'

'Oh, absolutely.'

On their way out, the doctor's secretary gave them directions to John Cary House, Katherine's ward.

'Who's John Cary?' said Penny as they turned onto a short path through the woods.

'No idea, love, you'll have to look him up in the school library.'

A slight grey-skinned man in a baggy grey suit and tweedy bedroom slippers stood guard at the door of John Cary House. They hadn't intended to go in, but as Penny and JJ approached the man swung the door open for them, so JJ took it as an unspoken invitation to enter. He heard Penny's objection, but knew she would follow rather than be left outside alone. They stood just inside the door, by a glass-fronted but vacant office, wondering what to do next, when a nurse appeared and asked if they needed help.

'We've come to see Katherine Jacobs,' said JJ.

'Are you family?'

'Yes, I'm her husband, and this is her daughter.'

'Just a minute please.' The nurse opened the office door and inspected a clipboard hanging on the wall before returning to them. 'I'm sorry, Mr Jacobs, but Katherine is not receiving visitors at the moment. And I think she's out at Discussion Group this afternoon in any case.'

'What do you mean, "not receiving visitors"?' he said. 'She's not the bloody Queen. I want to see my wife.'

'Dad!' Penny tugged at his arm. 'Dad, come on, we knew that.'

The nurse stood firm and said she was sorry but she would have to ask them to leave. A male nurse with red hair was hovering in a doorway behind her. Keeping an eye on things.

'Are you throwing me out?' said JJ.

'No, I'm asking you to leave.'

'And what if I refuse to go?'

'Then I'll throw you out.' She smiled.

'For god's sake, Dad. We'll miss the bus and have to walk.'

JJ was beaten. He knew he had no right to be there, or to threaten the people who were there to care for Katherine. He raised his hands in surrender, whispered an apology, but then a woman whisked in from nowhere and twirled around him, preventing his retreat to the door, where Penny was waiting for him.

'Stephanie, please let the gentleman leave,' said the nurse.

'SalomeSalomeSalome,' said Stephanie, wagging a finger in his face. She blew JJ a kiss as she danced off around the corner.

JJ and Penny set off in silence to catch the bus with JJ's outburst hanging between them like a fog of guilt and embarrassment that would not lift.

'What did the doctor mean about Mum being confused about Phoenix's death?'

'I'm not sure.'

125

'Then why didn't you ask?'

As they rushed towards the bus stop, they overtook the old man in the baggy suit and slippers, his hands clasped together behind his back as he shuffled along the road.

The old man stopped and pointed as they passed and JJ wished him a good evening.

'There's bears in they woods,' he said. 'Polar bears.'

'*Are* there?' said JJ.

'You want to come and see the bears?'

'Not today thanks, we'll miss our bus.'

***

THE CHRISTMAS BEFORE LAST, KATHERINE HAD been driving home from Bristol, where she'd been delivering presents, and was waiting at the top of a hill to turn left onto the main road. A cyclist appeared from her right and, nervous that she might be about to pull out in front of him, made deliberate eye contact. She smiled her acknowledgement as he sailed by, then turned to follow him down the hill. The straps of his pannier were flapping loose and she watched them, worried they might catch in his rear wheel. She remembered thinking the road must be travelling due west because the sun was low and in direct alignment with the road. The cyclist turned his head to one side, as if he'd been distracted by a shout, or maybe because the sun was blinding him, and crashed headlong into the rear end of a parked car. The force of the collision hurled him, a heavy middle-aged man, a poleless pole-vaulter, over the parked car's roof, tossing him head first onto the grass verge.

Katherine had pulled up alongside a telephone box a little further down the road and dialled 999. As she walked back to the scene of the accident, others were gathering: an old man who had been putting his dustbin out, still carrying its fluted metal lid like a shield; a woman who had been walking her small child in the park. Witnesses.

Katherine covered him with her overcoat, drawn the collar of it up to his chin as she had once tucked her children in at bedtime. He wasn't dead when the ambulance arrived but his eyes were bruised dark purple and swollen shut and blood was running from his nose, collecting in the well of his ear. He stirred when the ambulance men shouted questions at him, but died later in the hospital. She was the last person to have looked into his eyes, was the last to have seen and be seen by this man, this stranger with whom she had shared a final moment of intimacy. And what about her son, her beloved Phoenix? Had he shared a similar moment with the driver of the van that hit him?

A shout came from another room, from somewhere behind the sage green walls, reminding her where she was. The doctor had asked her a question and was waiting, eyebrows raised, for a response.

'Sorry,' she said. 'Come again?'

The doctor repeated his question in the level tones of someone trained beyond impatience. 'When we spoke yesterday, you told me that you and John had invented a second child, and that John had decided to kill him off, to uninvent him if you like, without your agreement. Is that correct?'

'No, it was the first child we made up, the eldest one.'

'Now Katherine, can you tell me why you might do that, invent a child?'

'Because of *Who's Afraid of Virginia Woolf?*' She began to sing, because mad people always sing and she wanted to be sure this doctor diagnosed her as such: '*Who's afraid of Virginia Woolf, Virginia Woolf, Virginia Woolf.*' Having observed the other patients on the ward, she'd worked out that it wasn't necessary to be too extreme to be accepted.

'I see. Is it the play you are referring to?'

'Yes, the play. Or the film.'

'Ah yes. I saw an excellent production of it at the Old Vic some time ago,' he said. 'Now, when I saw John yesterday he told me that you also had a real-life son who passed away recently. Is this son the same as the one you say you invented?'

'We didn't invent him, he was real.'

'Katherine. Is it too painful to talk about your son's death? Is that why you said you made him up?'

'No. Because he killed him.'

'Who killed who, Katherine?

'JJ, John, killed our son. Phoenix.'

'Are you able to tell me the exact circumstances of your son's death? How did Phoenix die?' The doctor rubbed his neat chin; he really was a dapper man.

'He was killed by a van.'

'And the van was driven by John?'

'No, but it's his fault Phoenix is dead; he encouraged him to get the bloody motor bike.'

As she spoke Katherine caught sight of the gardens for the first time, turned her head towards the window and there they were: neat lawns tinged with frost, hard round rose-beds, manicured with the precision of new graves. The doctor was watching her, watching her doing nothing, unable even to see from his side of the room what had caught her eye. He waited for her to turn her head back to him before speaking again. She wondered if he would have been as patient if she'd held that position for the whole interview.

'Katherine,' he said. 'Is there some way your son's death might be considered an accident?'

She pretended to consider his point but her response was unequivocal. 'No.'

The doctor pulled himself up straight in his chair and glanced at his watch. 'I'm afraid, Katherine,' he said, 'that's all we have time for today. I have arranged for you to be transferred out of Admissions and onto another ward this afternoon. In the meantime you should get some rest. Is that all right?'

Katherine nodded.

'Is there anything you would like to ask me about our chat today?'

She wanted to know how long she could stay, but like a child trying to stretch out the time before bed, decided that if she kept quiet he might forget that she had somewhere else to go, so she shook her head, too tired anyway to think or speak, now that rest had been suggested. At least she had secured herself another twenty-four hours away from home.

Her transfer from Admissions to John Cary House took her under orange lamps beside low red-brick buildings and onto a short narrow path through dense woodland. She was already light-headed from her medication and as she inhaled her first lungfuls of fresh air in thirty-six hours she felt giddy and needed to steady herself by clutching at the arm of the nurse accompanying her to the new ward.

They emerged from the woods and crossed the road to a semicircular driveway, climbed a short ramp to a door and let themselves in. The nurse rapped at a long window to attract the attention of another, younger, nurse who was sitting hunched over a desk, not working but picking at a white-bread sandwich. The young nurse looked up, smiled and pointed them towards a door marked *Office*.

'In we go,' said Katherine's nurse.

'Hello there. Is this Katherine Jacobs?'

'Say hello.' The nurse prompted Katherine as she might

a shy five-year-old arriving late to a birthday party.

'Yes,' said Katherine, and held out a hand.

'Hello Katherine, I'm Nurse Andrews - Sally. Welcome to John Cary House.' She took Katherine's outstretched hand and shook it.

'Well, I'll leave you here then, Katherine,' said the nurse from Admissions. 'Look after yourself.'

It was just a figure of speech, such as people bandy around when they can think of nothing else to say, but these were ominous words when spoken to someone whose greatest wish was to be looked after and to never have to do anything for herself ever again. To never again have to think about the shifts and troubles of life.

'Now, Katherine,' said the nurse. 'I have a suitcase here of your things. If you could write your name here for me we can make a list of its contents, and then I'll show you to your room. If you have any valuables or money it's best to leave them in here where they can be locked away safely for you. Is that okay? Hopefully we'll get everything done before the tea trolley arrives. I expect you could do with a cup of tea.'

Katherine nodded. There was no need to ask how her suitcase had got there. It was packed with all the clothes that JJ liked best, including the hideous silk blouse he'd bought her for Christmas, everything folded into neat squares. On top of it all was a flat brown envelope, her name written in blotched ballpoint on it. Katherine picked it out of the case and handed it to the nurse. 'I don't want this.'

131

'I'll lock it away with your valuables.'

'I'd rather you burned it.'

'I'm not allowed to do that. We'll put it away for now in case you want to look at it some other time.'

Katherine snatched it back, ripped it in half, then into smaller irregular squares that, by the time the nurse grabbed her wrist, scattered over her shoes like makeshift confetti.

'I'll have to report this to Doctor Wild,' said the nurse, as she dragged a metal wastepaper bin from under the desk and placed it next to Katherine's left leg. 'You can put the pieces in there, then we'll get on with our list.'

One by one the contents of the case were noted down. Underneath the top two layers of clothes, which included a short lilac negligee and a full-length flannelette nightdress, neither of which belonged to her, was a pile of books, all plays: *Virginia Woolf*, an early gift from JJ and inscribed 'from your favourite sparring partner'; *Godot*, *Death of a Salesman*, *Saved* and *Medea*. Obvious choices.

Sandwiched between them was a colour photograph of the family on holiday in France. They'd known at the time that it was likely to be Phoenix's last family holiday, but had had no inkling that death would be the reason for his future absence. It showed them all seated outdoors at a restaurant, their smiling faces shining like pomegranates in the evening sunshine, holding up glasses of vin rouge, Penny's watered-down toast pinker and thinner than the others, up to the camera - *Cheers*! Katherine passed the photograph to the nurse without comment.

JJ had always been a better packer than her, and this time he had excelled himself; each item in the case came with an invisible message attached: *please forgive me*, they begged.

The contents of her purse were meagre: two one-pound notes and thirty-six new pence in change. Still the nurse made a note of every penny and placed the purse in a large brown envelope.

'Have you no rings or jewellery? A watch?'

'No.' Her watch - rarely worn because its expanding metal bracelet bit at the hairs on her wrist like stinging ants - was in the Mini, abandoned somewhere near Weston-Super-Mare. And she and JJ had exchanged meaningful books and symbolic poetry in preference to matching rings and empty vows.

The clock on the wall showed twenty to six. Katherine signed her name at the bottom of the list and the nurse dropped it, with Katherine's chequebook, into the envelope. The butterfly clip was twisted and flattened and Katherine signed again on the outside.

'If you need money for the phone or the shop, just ask any of the staff and we can get it for you. Now let's take your things up to your room before tea.'

Out in the corridor the theme from *The Magic Roundabout* was blaring out from somewhere and someone was singing along: *da da da da da, d-d-d-da da*. The nurse locked the office door then hurried Katherine along: 'You'll meet everyone at teatime.' But Katherine wasn't bothered about meeting anyone, too busy wondering if it was always so noisy. The nurse led the way up to the first floor.

No one had told her she'd have a room to herself. It was small but with a large sash window. The walls were the same dirty apricot gloss that had flowed through the downstairs corridor and up the stairs, the carpet the same dark red cord, a bad colour for a carpet. Her room was furnished with a single, narrow iron-framed bed, beside which stood a teak locker with a drawer above and cupboard below. A moss-coloured easy chair that she knew she'd never sit in was squeezed into the space under the window between the washbasin and the wardrobe.

'You can unpack later,' said the nurse, helping Katherine to lift her case onto the bed. 'It's teatime now.'

Downstairs, they walked through a sitting room dominated by a large box of a television, the source of the noise, and a semicircle of armchairs. There was nobody watching but for one woman, who wasn't watching but spinning and weaving in and out and around the scattered chairs.

'Tea's here, Stephanie, come and eat,' said the nurse.

'SalomeSalomeSalome,' corrected the dervish woman, wagging a finger as she wove and waltzed her way through the door that led into the dining room, leaving a heady waft of cheap perfume in her wake that reminded Katherine of Penny.

Here there were people, hovering men and women. People sitting and standing at or around the formica-topped tables, smoking, muttering, waiting, twitching, in a semblance of a queue. One by one they disappeared then re-emerged through a side door carrying trays of food. There was something comforting in the timetabled institution of it, as if the bricks and mortar of the building were not solid after all but the expanding, interlocking sections of a safety net that she had jumped into from a great height. Nurse Sally Andrews explained the procedure and Katherine took her place at the back of the queue. They could be teachers, these people; this could be the staff dining-room at school, with one blissful difference, that nothing was expected of her here.

Katherine took her meal - mashed potato, peas, carrots, home-made steak and kidney pie and gravy, a school dinner but better cooked - and sat down in the first empty seat she came to, opposite a woman of fifty or so, who wore the sides of her long, well-groomed grey hair swept back off her face and tied behind. A black polo neck sweater and pale smooth complexion threw into relief her red beacon of a mouth, which parted as she smiled to reveal a row of square, even, yellow teeth.

'Hello dear, are you new here?'

'Yes, hello.' Katherine extended a hand across the table.

The woman took Katherine's one hand in both her own and inspected it. Her fingernails were long and painted red to match her lipstick and were not, as Katherine might have expected, picked at by anxiety or peeling with neglect, but pristine.

'Lovely, beautiful,' said the woman, turning Katherine's hand over. 'I'm going home tomorrow,' she said, as if she had somehow divined that information from Katherine's palm; Katherine pulled her hand free and the other woman picked up her cutlery, showing no sign of offence if any had been taken.

'What's your name?' Katherine asked the woman.

'Catherine, dear. And you?'

'Yes, Katherine.'

The woman, the other Catherine, frowned a moment and then laughed. 'Oh how funny. That just goes to prove I'm going home tomorrow.' Raising her voice, she announced: 'Here's another, more beautiful Katherine come to take my place.'

Katherine sneaked a look behind her but no one was paying them any attention. Catherine raised her knife and fork in one hand as if in toast and said, 'Welcome Katherine! How nice of you to come.' Then she started to eat, her actions measured and dignified. If it weren't for her age, and the colour of her teeth, she might be mistaken for a member of the royal family. Margaret, or Anne maybe.

So enamoured was she of her new surroundings, her refuge, that Katherine was blind to its reality. She and her fellow patients were guests at a country hotel; where bleating, grunting, jigging and farting were all tolerated, if not overlooked altogether.

She refused to take a Mogadon tablet that first night at John Cary House and regretted it later, in the dead of night, when she lay on her side in the bed, eyes fixed on the crack of light that shone under her door. Her whole mouth seemed to be coated with a substance that she imagined was waxy and white like glue and her tongue was stuck to the roof of her mouth.

Two shadows flickered across the bottom of the door, one after the other in quick succession: two feet or two people? Katherine groaned. Off in the distance a door squeaked open and shut again. Katherine smacked her lips, but no moisture could be summoned from anywhere. Her bladder was full. She was too tired to get out of bed to deal with either problem. She groaned again. The shadows reappeared and stopped. Her door opened a few inches. Katherine grunted as a nurse-shaped shadow slid into the room. She blinked in the light and her mouth clicked open again as she pushed herself up onto one elbow.

'What are you doing awake?' whispered the nurse. 'It's three o'clock. Do you need the toilet?' And in response to Katherine's nodding: 'Come on then.'

Katherine struggled out from under the blankets and the nurse helped her to her feet.

'Do you know where it is?'

Katherine nodded again. With one eye shut and the other half open, she squinted out into the corridor and felt her way along to the toilet while the nurse watched, waiting to finish her rounds.

Katherine sat on the toilet nodding, eyes closed, as her

pee corkscrewed into the water below.

'Okay?' said the nurse as she escorted her back along the corridor.

At the sink in her room she tipped her toothbrush out of its plastic beaker and gulped down a few mouthfuls of cold water. The water slid over whatever it was that coated her tongue and palate, so she held the next mouthful and swished it around but still it didn't penetrate; as soon as she swallowed the dryness returned. And already she could feel a renewed discomfort in her bladder. She refilled the beaker and placed it on the bedside table and climbed back into bed. The nurse had gone, leaving the door wide open, but she must have been listening out, for when the bed frame creaked she reappeared. 'Get back to sleep now,' she said.

'May I have a tablet?'

'Not now, I'm afraid, it's too late,' said the nurse. 'You won't wake up for breakfast.'

Katherine had no problem with missing breakfast, but she remembered her agreement with the consultant, that she was there to rest but there was to be no lying around in bed, so she lay down like a good girl, shut her eyes and tried to conjure up an image of her son's face. She could hear his voice calling her name from some distant place, but could not see him. It was important not to forget. She hadn't gone there to forget, but to remember, only to remember.

When morning came she could hardly rouse herself, her mouth was dry, her bladder full and although this awakening was a repeat of her earlier one she had no memory of having woken in the night. She pulled her dressing gown from the back of the door, wrapped it around herself and set off in search of a warm drink to penetrate whatever it was that was clogging her mouth. There was no one in sight upstairs and no sound from downstairs.

Two nurses sat in the office, hunched over the same something on the desk. One was talking and the other nodding. Katherine stood watching them when a waft of cold air hit her bare calves as the door opened behind her. A woman in a blue overall battled with the door's self-closing mechanism to lug an industrial vacuum cleaner through. Katherine moved aside to let her in, glimpsing a segment of grey sky as the door shunted itself closed.

'Hoover on Combe was broken so they hi-jacked ours,' the woman said. 'Forgot to bring it back, accidentally on purpose, like.' She rolled her eyes and smiled at Katherine.

Katherine smiled back then pushed the door open and the cold hit her face like a splash of icy water as she took a few steps down the ramp for her first impression of Barrow by daylight. She crossed the narrow road and turned to look back at the building that was her new home. A winter-stripped weeping willow grew out of a circle of stiff white grass in front of the door. Behind her, a path through the trees led to a distant opening where the frosted roofs of low buildings shimmered in the grey morning light. Trees everywhere, in all directions.

'There you are,' said a voice behind her. The nurse crossed over to stand at her side. 'Doesn't it look pretty?' she said, and Katherine agreed. It was a scene to define a season.

'Come in, you'll catch your death. Breakfast'll be here soon.'

Katherine watched the nurse's words float off in the mist that puffed from her mouth and realized how much comfort was to be drawn from the inane phrases she had always sneered at as meaningless: look after yourself, watch your step, in your own time.

'Come on, it's freezing,' said the nurse, from the door.

Inside, other people were coming downstairs, patients and staff.

'Have you had a wash?' said the nurse.

'I usually wash after breakfast.'

'All right, most people wash and dress before breakfast here, but you do what feels comfortable.'

Katherine knew that the next day she would conform to the behaviour of the majority, because that was what she was there for.

Music was playing from a white box fixed to the sitting-room wall. A choir of smarmy voices sang a jingle; *beebeecee*, ascending, *raydeeotooo*, riding a wave.

Men and women entered the dining room from opposite directions, approaching each other across the floor as if lining up for a session of country dancing. A few people waited in the sitting room, puffy-faced, piggy-eyed people, people dragging on their first cigarette of the day.

Katherine stood at the back of the room, where condensation was clearing from the French windows in spreading quarter-circles, looking like mist rising from the formal gardens beyond. In the distance, beech hedgerows, still brown-leaved in late winter, defended the gardens from the encroaching woodland.

'Good morning, dear, did you sleep well?' Catherine's hand rested a moment on Katherine's sleeve, her pink nails - hadn't they been scarlet the evening before? - harsh against the floral delicacy of the flannelette. She was dressed in a silky blue blouse and grey tweed skirt, her make-up was fresh and the morning's ration of perfume was still so pungent as to be unidentifiable; Katherine swallowed the urge to splutter from its fumes.

'I'm going home today,' said the other Catherine.

'Are you?'

But the other Catherine had moved away, gone to perform the same routine with a man who was sitting, head in hands, elbows propped by the wooden arms of his chair, his balding crown pointing towards where Katherine stood by the window. He failed to respond, but Catherine moved on undeterred, like a bee gathering pollen, to a young girl so thin and gaunt she appeared haggard as a crone. Her long hair was tucked behind her ears but dangled in the path of her biro as she scribbled across the page of a notebook.

'Lovely. Bye then,' pre-empted the girl - just as Penny might do - with the insolence of youth, when Catherine's hand came to rest on her shoulder. The girl's clipped consonants and RP vowels were delivered by a voice surprisingly deep for one of so little physical substance.

'I'm going home today,' said Catherine, delivering her message regardless before moving on undaunted.

The breakfast trolley trundled through pulled by a tall, morose-looking man in a brown work coat. StephanieSalome danced in its wake as a seagull follows a trawler. 'Breakfast everyone,' she squawked and people shuffled towards the dining room.

Katherine hung back, as did the thin girl, whose scribbling had become more frantic. Pleasant as she was, Katherine wanted to wait until the other Catherine had collected her food and sat down before she took her place in the queue. Even if she was leaving that day, which Katherine doubted from the reactions of other patients to her news, she didn't want to set any difficult precedents so early in her stay.

'Fried or scrambled?' said the nurse serving the food.

Maybe it was the sight of the fried eggs afloat in a sea of grease or the smell of the food in general that triggered her nausea, but all of a sudden Katherine's appetite was gone, not that she'd been particularly hungry to begin with. 'Scrambled, please.'

Every table was already occupied by at least one person but for the one furthest away, next to the window. In a restaurant it would be the prime table, the one reserved for local celebrities, but at Barrow, as at school, the tables closest to the serving hatch filled first: get it down you while it's still warm, be first in line for second helpings.

She sat down in the chair with the view across the gardens, with her back to the room, and no sooner had she done so than a shadow clouded her peripheral vision; from its movement, she reckoned on it being StephanieSalome and her perpetually wagging finger so she busied herself with a close inspection of the food on her plate. When it felt safe to look up, she discovered that her audience had been not StephanieSalome but a taller, thinner woman whose blue-rinsed hair hovered about her face like an unruly and faded hydrangea. The woman's face was engaged in a one-woman gurning contest and beneath it a tea towel was tied under her chin like a bib.

The scribbling girl was led by the arm to collect her breakfast. She could weigh no more than five or six stone and her clothes drooped loose from the angles of her bony frame. Her eyes bulged. Katherine lowered her gaze and concentrated on directing her fork towards her mouth because, for some reason, her hands were shaking.

When she next looked up, the gurning woman was still hovering, but a male nurse with pale red hair was doing his best to manoeuvre her into what looked like an adult version of a high chair.

'Come on, Iris love,' he said. 'Help us out.'

143

Katherine marvelled at the appropriateness of her name; with her blue hair and trembling limbs she wouldn't be out of place at the marshy edge of a pond.

Iris emitted a frustrated guttural question, seemingly directed at Katherine. The nurse turned his head. 'Ah,' he said. 'A new face. Iris would like to be introduced,' he said to Katherine. 'Katherine, this is Iris; Iris, Katherine.'

Iris made a noise in the back of her throat, and Katherine realized she was expected to answer so she said 'Hello, pleased to meet you.'

'Now then, let's get you into this chair before your food goes cold,' said the nurse.

Katherine turned back to her own plate to find that the thin girl had slipped unseen and unheard into the seat opposite, presenting a ghoulish portrait against the window's frame. Downy white hair grew on her cheeks like a newborn baby. What little appetite Katherine had promptly vanished.

'She's got Parkinson's disease,' said the girl.

'Oh,' said Katherine. One of the Gingerbread mums had been diagnosed with early symptoms of Parkinson's just before Christmas and, what with everything, Katherine had forgotten to check how she was.

'Her mind is as sharp as a knife,' said the girl. 'But she can't control her body at all. She shits herself all the time.'

The girl saw someone coming towards them and shut up, took to reorganizing the food on her plate. The someone coming was the nurse with the morning drug ration.

'Two for you, Katherine,' she said. 'You haven't eaten much.'

'No,' said Katherine. 'I'm not all that hungry.'

'Just see if you can manage a bit more to help the tablets down. Now, Louisa, what about you?' she handed the girl her drugs.

'I'm not all that hungry either,' said Louisa.

'EAT!' said the nurse, and then turned back to Katherine, immediately softening her voice. 'The doctor would like you to stay on the ward this morning, and he'll be over to see you as soon as he can. All right?'

'All right,' said Katherine. The nurse moved on to the next table.

'Bitch,' said Louisa, and the nurse surely heard.

People took their pills, cleared their plates and drifted away from the dining room. Katherine returned to her room to wash and dress. Ignoring the suitcase of clean clothes that had been pushed under her bed, she dressed in the underwear and outer layers strewn over her chair from the night before.

Sitting on the edge of her bed to pull on her tights she closed her eyes and imagined the soft pillow under her head, wishing she could lie down and not get up for a week. It couldn't hurt to lie down for a few minutes. She dropped onto her side, her legs dangling over the side of the bed.

'Katherine!' She was being summoned; she had forgotten the doctor was coming, and had already broken the rules on her second day. But when she headed downstairs, a nurse was standing below holding a bouquet of scarlet roses. Katherine stopped on the stairs.

'Look what came for you,' said the nurse.

'I don't want them.'

'It's Valentine's Day soon,' said the nurse, as if that information would make a difference to anything.

'I don't want them.' Katherine walked past her without taking the flowers. 'You can put them in the bin.'

'I can't do that, they're for you, from your husband.'

'Then send them back. Tell him to put them on my son's grave.'

'I could put them in the lounge for everyone to enjoy?'

Katherine turned back, snatched the bouquet and pushed against the outside door. She strode across to the edge of the woods and pitched a long overarm throw, tossing the flowers into the woods, like a bride at a wedding attended only by trees. Without waiting to see where they landed, she returned to the ward, past the dumbfounded nurse to the sitting room that smelled of fried food and cigarette smoke. She chose an armchair near the French windows and sat down to wait for the doctor.

By Saturday lunchtime, Katherine had overcome her repulsion at Louisa's physical state helped by the fact that she was the only other person on the ward able or willing to hold a decent conversation; so they were sharing what had become their table for the fourth day in a row.

'How old are you?'

'Seventeen.'

'You're midway between my two children.'

This information elicited no response from Louisa, so Katherine continued. 'My son's dead. Which is why I'm here I suppose.'

'Did you kill him?'

'Of course not.'

'My parents won't even come here when I'm alive, so there's no way they'd be here if I died. In fact they've probably forgotten I'm here, so I might as well be dead. One institution or another, as long as I'm safely locked up it's all the same to them.'

'But you're not locked up here.'

'That's what they tell you. Have you tried leaving?'

'Well, no,' said Katherine. 'Why are you here?'

'School matron. Said I wasn't eating enough.'

'You are very slim.'

'No I'm not! Look at this.' Louisa lifted her jumper and grabbed a tiny pinch of skin between finger and thumb. 'Pure fat,' she said.

Katherine thought it best not to comment. One of her pupils had been anorexic and Katherine had decided to treat her the same as everyone else and let the professionals handle her. She glanced over at Louisa's plate, where a single chip had been separated from the rest and sliced into tiny pieces; Louisa hadn't eaten anything yet, just

147

moved things around and chopped them up to make the portions seem smaller.

'Where are your parents?'

'Middle East. Father's a Major in the army. They're in Sharjah now; I've never been there. Which is better than when I was younger and they were in Caracas and they kept ferrying me back and forth on the lollipop flights. At least I don't have to do that any more.'

Across the way, Iris was being fed at her low high chair, a tea towel tucked in the neck of her lilac twin set. One nurse held her head still while the male nurse attempted to spoon puréed shepherd's pie into her mouth and Iris strained to control her swallow reflex. It was painful to watch, like most things on the ward became painful to watch the more you saw them, even Stephanie/Salome's dancing, which was why, Katherine decided, Gordon the head-in-hands man maintained that same pose even when he needed to use his hands to eat.

Louisa nodded towards Katherine's empty plate. 'Do you want some more? I'm full.'

Katherine refused. It was not her responsibility to tell the girl to eat; if she were home and the girl was Penny it would be, if they were at school and the girl were one of her pupils it might be, but at John Cary House all responsibility was deferred. But she wasn't going to eat for her.

'You'd better eat up, Louisa, or we'll be over to you next,' said the male nurse feeding Iris.

148

Louisa picked up her fork and recommenced the rearrangement of the food on her plate. Katherine went in search of tea to wash down her midday pills and when she returned it did appear that Louisa had eaten something, until she noticed a scattering of chips under the table. Katherine pointed to the notebook that occupied the space next to Louisa's plate at every meal.

'Do you mind if I ask what you're writing?'

'Nothing really,' said Louisa. 'A play.'

'A play? Really? That's not nothing. I adore plays. I'm a drama teacher. Do you have a favourite play, or playwright?'

'Not especially. I quite like Shakespeare.'

Katherine was disappointed, imagining the faux-classical language sandwiched between the covers of the notebook. Louisa had probably been privately educated in a stuffy institution that refused to recognize the existence of the hundreds and thousands of great writers who had processed through the theatre since Elizabethan times.

Louisa laid a protective hand on the cover of her book as if anticipating a lunge towards it by Katherine. 'I don't show it to anyone,' she said.

'Of course not,' said Katherine. 'All the best writers are secretive about their work. Some people believe the best writers are those who write purely for their own satisfaction rather than for public recognition, like the poet Emily Dickinson. Are you studying for A-levels?'

'I was.'

'LOUISA!'

Louisa picked up a chip with her fingers and nibbled at the end of it. The rest, she waved around like an aberrant finger as she spoke. 'Three,' she continued. 'Maths, physics, biology. I want to study physical education at college.'

Katherine diverted her surprise at the disparity between Louisa's rather obvious lack of physical strength with the demands her chosen future career would make upon her body into a feigned dashed expectation that she would be studying at least one arts subject. 'That's a very different occupation to writing,' she said. 'I started to write a play once.'

'What about?'

A teenage girl, as a matter of fact. Who escapes to England from Poland, from the Russian occupation at the end of the war. A kind of odyssey I suppose, only she travels away from the things she loves rather than towards them.' As Katherine talked she looked straight ahead, out of the window, but her peripheral vision caught Louisa checking no one was watching before grabbing another few chips from her plate to throw under the table. She noticed later that two of them had landed at the feet of a woman three tables away.

'Sounds good,' said Louisa. 'Why didn't you finish it?'

'I don't know. I suppose I didn't have time with two children to bring up.'

'You could do it in here,' suggested Louisa. 'It'd help ease the boredom. They leave you alone if you're writing too; they think it's cathartic. That's why I do it.' She pulled a skeletal grin and Katherine had never witnessed such a clear vision of living death. Even Phoenix had looked more alive in the Chapel of Rest. She looked across the room to where Iris was being cleaned up before being taken out for a spot of fresh air.

'I think I'll go for a walk too,' said Katherine, more to herself than to anyone else.

'I'm off to Discussion Group,' said Louisa. 'You should come; it's actually not bad. If no one has anything to talk about we play records. Which is all right as long as you like Don McLean.'

'Maybe I'll come next time,' said Katherine, suddenly desperate for some time to herself.

'All right. Come on Monday. I'll introduce you.'

Katherine wasn't sure she wanted to be introduced, but she thanked her anyway and picked up her plate, cup and saucer to return them to the kitchen. Yesterday's nurse was just coming on duty when Katherine went in search of her coat.

'Hello Katherine, where are you off to?'

'I'm going for a walk.'

'Good idea, get some air.'

'Yes. It's really smoky in there.'

'Do you want to take some money for the shop?'

'No, I don't think so, thank you.'

There were two other villas beside John Cary House - Combe and Blagdon - and from the outside they appeared identical. Combe was where all the meals were cooked and had a phone box outside for patients to use. Katherine was allowed to visit the other villas, but there was little point, as she knew nobody there. She set off to her left.

The road surface was made of yellow-tinted concrete scored with millions of horizontal ridges, which she imagined would make for a bumpy ride on a bicycle. When Penny was little she would have insisted on counting each ridge; JJ would have stood patiently waiting as she counted, while Katherine marched on ahead.

A green sign next to a weeping willow pointed to a prefabricated hut, the Occupational Therapy Unit, a sort of elongated Doghouse. Behind it, half-hidden behind a row of young conifers, was a large detached red brick house, with a white Austin Maxi and a child's red tricycle stationed in its driveway. Alongside the house, a muddy track travelled in the same direction as the sign that pointed the way to the hospital farm.

Soon, the buildings petered out and the road passed through dense woodland on either side. Besides the occasional passing car, Katherine saw no one. She trudged on until at last the woods opened out onto an expanse of grass where the first crocus and daffodil spears were poking through. A circle of snowdrops nodded in the shelter of yet another willow, next to a green bench, which had been positioned so that its occupant might choose a view of the main gates or, by a simple turn of the head, the tree. A small square plaque attached to the bench told her it had been donated to the hospital by the *Barrow Hospital League of Friends*. Some friends; presumably most patients didn't need to sit on a bench and stare at a weeping willow to be reminded of whatever sadness had brought them there. And Katherine had as much interest in watching the gates as she did in walking through them, so she passed on, keeping going until she came to a bus shelter with a bench in it and by then it was a relief to sit down and take a few moments to get her bearings. She had walked in a semicircle and if her calculations were correct, John Cary House would be somewhere behind the buildings immediately in front of her.

A youngish man with long loping strides bounced past, neck forward, shoulders hunched, one hand in his pocket, his other arm bent halfway up his back; a black Ford Escort indicated left and turned into a car park opposite the bus shelter; the young man strode by again in the other direction; a nurse emerged from a path out of the woods and bent down to retie a shoelace; there may have been half an hour between each of these events or they may have been consecutive.

'Excuse me,' said Katherine to the nurse. 'Which is the quickest way back to John Cary House?'

The nurse pointed out the route and Katherine thanked her then sat a while longer in the bus shelter, listening to the chatter of a single magpie.

The long-legged man approached for a third time but this time he broke his stride to come and sit next to her in the bus shelter. Keeping her eyes trained on the path that would take her back to the ward, she avoided his gaze. Something about her profile was fascinating to his slitty green eyes. When she at last gave in and turned towards him, his face contorted into a wild grin. Katherine smiled back; a smile designed to neither encourage nor offend. She stood and walked out of the bus shelter; he followed at a distance, but she knew he would catch her up. When he did he stretched out a hand for her to shake. She took it without gripping but he grasped hers and pulled it in to his chest; there was no violence in his action, it was a straightforward act of inappropriate love. He leaned a pockmarked face in towards her as if daring to plant a kiss on her cheek, but thought better of it and pulled away. He dropped her hand and ran off ahead onto the path through the woods. Katherine trailed behind, slowing her pace to see what he would do.

He leapt up to grab at a branch and then ran off into the woods on one side, his jacket billowing out behind him. He reappeared for a second, looking over his shoulder as if being chased by a wild animal visible only to himself, then vanished again into the trees on the other side. When he came crashing back through the undergrowth towards her, Katherine realized he was showing off for her benefit, but then he found the path again and ran away at full pelt, towards the road and out of sight. He didn't come back. Another mother's son.

Back on the ward the sitting room was deserted but for head-in-hands Gordon who sat not watching the horse racing on television with the volume at full blast. She toyed with the idea of challenging him to a game of Scrabble - he wouldn't have to shift position, she could slide the board into the space between his elbows - but instead she went in search of a glass of water to lubricate her parched mouth.

There's A Ghost In My House

THE MONDAY AFTER HALF TERM, PENNY ARRIVED home from school to find a box of groceries in the porch: six eggs, a Sunblest loaf in a waxy wrapper, four tins of beans, a pack of Wall's Best pork sausages, three tins of tomato soup, a five-pound bag of potatoes, eight apples in a brown paper bag, four oranges, a cabbage (nice try, Dad), a bag of carrots, one swede and some parsnips (ditto). Only four tins of cat food - she had given up telling him that if he took the car he could carry more - a tin of sardines and some mince in bloody paper, a lump of cheddar in greaseproof paper, two tins of tomatoes, a pack of spaghetti and a net of onions. The idea probably being that she should make spaghetti bolognese. She pushed the box into the kitchen with her feet and unloaded its contents, put the meat and cheese in the fridge and left the rest on the table.

She went up to her parents' bedroom to watch for the hospital bus. The girl was there as usual, half-leaning, half-sitting against the wall outside the Cider Institute reading, her bag slung on the ground by her feet. Penny saw the bus coming up from the village, its slow blinking indicator reflected in the road's wet surface. The girl must have recognized the sound of its engine because without looking up she shut her book onto her hand, picked up her bag and moved away from the wall and closer to the kerb. The bus stopped at four eighteen exactly and the girl disappeared into it.

Penny recast the scene in her mind with herself drawn into it, as she would be the next day when she went to visit her mother. The question was whether to get to the corner before or after the girl. If she was there first it might look as though she'd been there for hours not knowing what time the bus was due. The really smart thing would be to watch for the bus from the window as she had today, run like hell downstairs and out the front door, then stroll calmly over the road to the corner just as the bus pulled up. But knowing her luck, she'd fall off her platforms in the road and the bus would run her over, or else she'd get the timing all wrong and miss it altogether. Or else she'd fall down the stairs and break her neck and no one would find her for days until the stench finally penetrated out into the garden, overwhelmed the smell in the Doghouse and alerted JJ.

Everything was back to normal with Jackie. As Penny had hoped, their forthcoming holiday had replaced the Jackie and Phoenix problem as the uppermost matter on their collective mind. Positive had ousted negative. In fact, for Penny it had ousted a lot of negatives, none of which could ever be revealed to Jackie: her mum in the loony bin, her dad living like a tramp in the garden shed. Nothing like that would ever happen to Jackie's family. Even if Jackie died her parents would walk around the village hand in hand, red eyes hidden behind sunglasses, their grief lending them a glistening dignity. Life would go on, as everyone always says it must in such circumstances, and in a year or so's time Jackie's mum would be carrying a neat bump under a denim smock, because after all she was still young and her international secretarial career would still be there when Jackie mark two started school. She could use the break to brush up on her Esperanto.

At four sixteen the next day, the girl still hadn't taken up her position on the corner, and Penny was worried she might not be coming; maybe she had been struck down with something overnight. Rather than miss the bus herself she went out anyway. As it was the bus almost sailed past her because the girl was already on it and the driver wasn't expecting anyone to be waiting. With her face as red as the bus, Penny waited for the door to concertina open and climbed aboard.

'All right, love,' said the driver. 'You going up to the hospital?'

Too embarrassed to speak, Penny nodded and took a

seat at the front of the bus so she didn't have to walk past the other passengers, of which there were only two, the girl and a man with eyes like a cat. The front of the bus smelled of petrol and stale tobacco.

When the bus stopped to let the girl off, Penny watched, without being too obvious about it, as she crossed the road, waved to the driver and walked through the gate of the house opposite, number twelve.

'Where are you going to, love?' said the driver, speaking to Penny through his rearview mirror.

Penny blushed again. 'To visit my mum.'

'You getting off in the hospital grounds then?'

'Yes please,' said Penny.

The driver waved at the man in the gatehouse, and the man in the gatehouse didn't wave back. 'Miserable old sod,' said the driver, beaming round at Penny.

She didn't see Katherine at first because she was sitting on a bench in the corner of the bus shelter and didn't seem to be looking out for Penny; she didn't even get up when the bus pulled in. She didn't look any different.

'Mum,' said Penny.

'Hello,' said Katherine, turning but staying seated, so Penny sat down beside her and together they watched Mr Cat's Eyes lope off and disappear into a building opposite. The bus driver switched off his engine and left the bus, smiling and nodding at Penny as he passed. He turned onto a path that cut through the woods behind them, newspaper rolled under his arm, pipe stuck to his bottom lip.

'What shall we do then?' said Penny.

'What?'

'What shall we do? Is there somewhere we can go? It's cold out here.'

'I'll show you my room if you like.'

'All right.'

Katherine introduced Penny to the nurses on duty, although none of them by name, and it was obvious to all concerned that she couldn't remember any of them.

'Why don't you take Penny in for tea and biscuits?' suggested a pretty young nurse with a Welsh accent.

'I'd like to show her my room first,' said Katherine.

The nurse smiled at Penny and suggested they might want to come back down for tea afterwards rather than stay upstairs. The doctor had warned that Katherine might seem a little strange on account of the drugs.

'I've put the photo of you by my bed,' said Katherine.

Strange wasn't the word for it. When she spoke she seemed normal, just a bit slower, but what was really mental was the way she behaved as if she and Penny were close and that this visit was a simple continuation of their ongoing intimacy. But you never could tell when Katherine was acting.

Penny looked closer at the photograph on the bedside table; it had been folded in half so that only Penny and

Katherine were visible from the bed. Phoenix and JJ were folded around the back and provided the ballast to hold the card upright like a greetings card. Mental.

'Look, we've got tennis courts,' said Katherine, pointing out of the window.

A subtle blend of poo, sick and bleach in the general atmosphere made the small room twice as claustrophobic as it would otherwise have been and Penny was beginning to feel queasy.

'Great,' said Penny. 'Can we go down for tea now? I haven't had anything since lunchtime, I'm starving.'

Katherine turned away from the window without saying anything and led the way out.

'That's Louisa's room,' she said, touching a door as they passed.

'Who's Louisa?'

'She's out at Discussion Group. I left early to meet you. She may be back before you go. You might like her, she's seventeen.'

What was she doing in a mental home at that age? Penny hadn't realized you could go mad as young as that.

'I think she's anorexic,' said Katherine, lowering her voice.

They went into a large sitting room where a radio was playing too loud for normal conversation, but at least the fog of cigarette smoke cancelled out the foul smell. A memory flashed into Penny's mind of Phoenix brandishing a box of matches that he was taking with him to the toilet to eliminate the smell he was about to make.

A blue-haired woman stood quivering in the centre of the room, listening, a slow yellow-brown rivulet snaking from under her skirt and down her bare leg, staining the top of her rolled-down stocking.

'This way,' said Katherine, and Penny followed her into the dining room.

The man who'd seen the nurse threaten to throw JJ out was sitting talking to a cleaning lady who waved a fag around as she spoke. His conspiratorial smile suggested that Katherine had been told nothing of JJ's embarrassing outburst and Penny's confirmed in return that she wouldn't be the one to spill the beans.

'Go and sit over there.' Katherine pointed to a table by the window.

As Penny watched her mother return with two cups of tea rattling in their saucers she tried to remember the last time she had had a cup of tea delivered to her by her mother. It just wasn't something Katherine did.

'Will you come again tomorrow?' said Katherine, before she'd even sat down. 'I'm not all that keen on Discussion Group so it's a real treat to have an excuse to leave early.'

'If I can,' said Penny. 'We're going on a school outing tomorrow to the Arnolfini so it depends what time we get back.'

'Will you bring me something? On the top shelf of my wardrobe is a shirt box, white with blue squiggles on it.

Will you bring it for me?' She whispered across the table as if asking Penny to smuggle her in a crate of whiskey.

'What, the whole thing? What's in it?'

'Yes, I need it all. You can look if you like. It's not heavy and I can meet you at the bus stop again.'

They sat in silence for several minutes sipping their tea, until a wailing sound started up in the sitting room and Penny's alarm must have shown on her face.

'That's Iris singing,' said Katherine. 'Poor dear. She can hardly control any part of herself any more. Nothing wrong with her mind though. It's very sad.'

'Then why isn't she in a normal hospital?'

'Because the treatment they give her makes her depressed, so she comes in here for that. It's better for her in here in any case, she can have more freedom and the nurses take her out for little walks. Don't you think the grounds are lovely? I might take her out in the wheelchair,' she said, drifting off mid-sentence as if trying to remember what it was that prevented her making a final decision on the matter. Penny was tempted to ask, but Katherine had already changed the subject. 'Do you know,' she said, 'there are orchids growing out the back there in the garden that you won't see anywhere else in the country, growing wild? No one sees them but the people here.'

'What colour are they?' said Penny, for want of something to say. She had never seen an orchid.

'No one knows. They won't flower until spring.'

'Someone must have seen them,' said Penny. 'Otherwise how do they know they're there at all?'

But Katherine's attention had drifted again. Other patients were arriving back from wherever they had spent the afternoon. Someone switched the television on without turning the radio off first. Penny heard the chiming theme of Crossroads. Five twenty-five.

'Can we watch the first half of *Crossroads*, before I go?'

They went into the sitting room and Penny sat down next to the most normal-looking of the residents, a woman wearing bright red lipstick, who greeted her with a smile and the information that she was going home the next day. Penny smiled back then turned to her mother, who was standing behind her for some reason, with her hands on the back of her chair.

'Mum, can we switch the radio off?'

'Iris, this is my daughter Penny. Do you mind if we turn the music off while we watch *Crossroads*? Would you like to sit down and watch it with us?' Katherine hadn't forgotten how to use her teacher's voice. Iris made glottal noises and waggled her arms in response. 'Thank you,' said Katherine.

Penny tried to concentrate on what was happening at the Crossroads Motel, but the sight of her mother helping Iris into a chair was too much of a distraction and Penny winced each time her mother came close to touching the streaks of liquid poo drying on Iris's leg.

The commercial break came and with it, time for Penny

to catch the bus home. It was getting dark outside. 'Mum, will you walk to the bus stop with me?'

'Of course.'

The shirt box Katherine wanted was full of scraps of old rubbish: the photograph of Katherine towering above her school friends that JJ would fish out whenever Penny got upset about her height to reassure her that Katherine had been tall too and she'd turned out all right (he'd never be able to pull that one again); foreign bus or train tickets, Penny couldn't tell which, and nor did she care; a white oval pebble; an unposted postcard of the Rijksmuseum in Amsterdam with two lines written in Polish on the back; a newspaper clipping in Polish; a photo of a man and a woman, the Polish grandparents she had never met, who looked like her mother only with longer pointier faces, waving hello from under a tree in Poland; and endless scraps of paper torn from notebooks with odd paragraphs or sentences or sometimes just single words written on them, some in English, some in Polish, all in her mother's handwriting.

Underneath it all was a foolscap notebook with *The Wrong Height*, also in her mother's handwriting, written on the cover. Penny flicked through pages and pages of notes. Some of it was set out like a play but most of it was set out more like a diary. Either way, it was illegible and Penny buried it again under the loose stuff and replaced the lid.

She took the box down to the kitchen and found an

old shopping bag under the sink to put it in along with the book she was reading (*The Female Eunuch*, a birthday present from JJ) ready for her to take the next day.

There was no light on in the Doghouse. Too hungry to wait for JJ to bring fish and chips she emptied a tin of beans into a pan - JJ had been known to stand the actual tin on the hotplate, like cowboys used to, he said - and settled down in front of the TV to watch Top of the Pops.

'It's making me seasick,' said Penny.

Jackie's response was a forced grunt. This was not like Jackie; art was her best subject, she loved it, had got a grade A in the mocks and was the best artist in their year by miles. They were standing in front of Cataract 3, one of the exhibits in the Bridget Riley exhibition. The principle disadvantage of any school outing was being marched by nuns past the Dug Out, even if it was the middle of the day and there was no one there to see them. The saving grace was that like the entrance to all mythical places the door to the Dug Out was invisible in daylight; no matter how many times Penny walked up and down the hill on a Saturday she could never spot the entrance, whereas at night it was obvious on account of the brick shithouse of a doorman who guarded it.

Granted, she had only been there once, one Saturday night last year when she'd stayed over at Jackie's because Jackie's parents were away. The brick shithouse had overlooked their being underage, probably because of Penny's height and Jackie's pretty face and short skirt. Everything in the Dug Out was black: the walls, the floors, the people. A series of underground caverns connected by arches, it was as claustrophobic as hell, and filled with so much stinking smoke that you'd think someone had set fire to a pile of manure in there. Penny had to keep going to stand at the bottom of the narrow staircase until her breathing returned to normal.

Cataract 3 was having a similar affect on her. She made a quick note in her exercise book: *red, grey and turquoise waves, like the sea, or hills, or a wonkily ploughed field. Makes me seasick. When I shut my eyes I can still see it.* She moved on to the next picture.

'C'mon our Jack,' she said.

But Jackie's feet were rooted to the pale wooden floor, her legs were stiff, and the top half of her body was swaying backwards and forwards, in a motion that disagreed with the picture in front of her.

'MISS!' Penny knocked her funny bone on the wall as she lunged for Jackie who was about to pitch, straight-legged and face first, into the picture. 'MISS, JACKIE'S FAINTED!'

Sister Peter skipped across and draped Jackie's arm around her shoulders to support her. 'Please run and fetch a glass of water, Penelope,' she said. 'And bring it outside.'

Penny dashed to the café and begged a pint glass of water. When she found them again, Jackie was sitting up

169

with her head between her knees on the quayside cobbles. Anyone going by on a boat would be able to see right up her skirt, not that Jackie would mind, thought Penny, but the hypocrisy of the nuns made her laugh. On the one hand, there was an actual school rule that disallowed them wearing patent shoes because anyone looking at them closely enough would be able to see the reflection of their uptheskirt region, but here was Sister Peter letting Jackie flash her fanny at half of Bristol.

'Here you are, miss,' said Penny, handing her the glass.

'It's not for me,' said the nun. 'Give it to Jacqueline. Didn't they have anything smaller?'

Penny shrugged. 'I thought you might need a lot, to pour over her head or something.'

'I see,' said the nun. 'Well, it's for drinking. Do you know which is Jacqueline's coat? Please go and fetch it from the cloakroom.'

Jackie was shivering with cold and shock as she revived. Penny ran off and did as she was told, anything was better than going back into the exhibition; she raised a V-sign to the other girls as she passed the gallery. 'She nearly died,' she said. 'I saved her.' They all knew it was a lie, but they loved it.

When she came back with the coat, Sister Peter was helping Jackie to her feet. Penny threw the coat over her friend's shoulders and took her free arm. In her opinion Jackie was laying it on a bit thick.

'We'll go into the cafeteria,' said Sister Peter. 'And you

may stay with her, Penelope, until we are ready to leave.' Sister Peter sent Penny on ahead with a pound note and over-enunciated instructions to buy Jackie a sandwich and a cup of tea sweetened with three spoonfuls of sugar. As soon as Penny arrived at the table with the tray, Sister Peter rushed off to supervise the other girls. All the gold had gone from Jackie's complexion.

'That was weird,' she said. 'At first it looked like a load of waves, all moving in the same direction, but then it changed into hundreds of mouths all opening and closing at different times.'

'What were they saying?'

'Nothing, moron, it was just an optical conclusion.'

They both laughed, back to normal, taking the piss out of Elizabeth Andrews, the class pedant, who managed to get her words twisted almost as often as her knickers. They passed the tea and the cheese-and-pickle sandwich back and forth between them, and even though she was glad Jackie was okay, Penny couldn't help but be jealous of her for fainting. Somehow she always managed to do the glamorous thing. For Penny to draw that much attention to herself she would have to fake it, and everyone would know. Even if it were for real, it would be about as glamorous as the felling of a tree; someone would shout TIMBER! as she went down, and onlookers would scatter to avoid being crushed, and they'd have to drag her out by her feet because no one was strong enough to lift her.

Penny's consolation prize was not having to go back into the exhibition, although no doubt she would still be expected to write an essay on what little of it she had seen. And there was one other benefit by proxy to come; due to Jackie's fragile state, the two of them were allowed to catch the bus home from Colston Green instead of traipsing all the way back up the hill to school first, so Penny was home in plenty of time to change out of her uniform before catching the hospital bus.

There was no sign of JJ. It was probably deadline day again, as it seemed to be every day nowadays. The Mini was gone and the Doghouse was cold.

A note pinned to the back door told her he would be out late, that she was to sort out her own tea (as if she didn't every day), and that he'd have fish and chips (again) in town. He'd left her the newspapers in the back porch with the usual squares cut out and strips dangling, the telly page intact. Penny was disappointed not to be able to share the fainting story with him; he always enjoyed hearing about Jackie's film-starry calamities. She'd have to make do with telling her mum and suffering her underwhelming response.

The Barrow bus girl arrived at her corner earlier than usual; perhaps she was living a parallel existence to Penny, perhaps her best friend had fainted on a school outing and they'd also been sent home early. Not much benefit in it for her though as the final stage of her journey was dependent on that one bus and all it meant was that she got to spend an extra twenty minutes sitting on the cold wall. Penny considered calling her over for a cup of tea, but if she didn't like her then she'd be stuck with having to talk to her every time she went to visit Katherine, so she dismissed the idea.

At ten past four, when Penny crossed the road, the girl didn't so much as look up. But then she did.

'Excuse me,' she said. 'Do you mind if I ask you a question?'

'No,' said Penny.

'Do you know Mrs Jacobs? It's just that you look like her, a younger version.'

'She's my mother.'

'Really? I knew it. You're so lucky? She's my favourite teacher. And I hate drama, so that's saying something.'

'Me too,' said Penny. 'Can't stand it. All my mum reads is plays. I like more political stuff.'

'Do you? I've never read anything political. What are you reading now?'

'Something called *The Female Eunuch*. I've only just started it, but it's great.' Penny pulled the book from her bag and showed her the cover.

'Right, I read about that. There was a review in *The Guardian* a while ago. The bus is coming.'

Penny flicked through *The Guardian* every day, after JJ had finished with it, but only in search of news of Gary or Marc or David (of which there was very little, the *Mirror* was better for the kind of information Penny wanted).

The girl must be very sophisticated to read not only obscure books but also articles about books. More like the daughter Katherine could love. The conversation was forgotten thanks to the appearance of a green double-decker that must have been taken out of public service at least fifty years before.

The girl went onto the lower deck and sat down with her back to the window and her legs stretched out along the width of the seat, so Penny did the same a few seats away.

'Are you visiting someone at the hospital?' Said the girl.

There was no need to be so direct. What should Penny say to this girl who knew her mother? If she told the girl that her drama teacher was in the loony bin, it would be safe to presume it would be all over the Comprehensive the next day. The bus was only just beginning its slow chug uphill, it would be ambitious to try to delay her answer until the girl had to get off; she would appear stupid, struggling with a question that required only a straight yes or no answer, not really anything to think about. So she said yes and hoped the girl wouldn't pursue it further. Some hope.

'It's not your mum, is it? I noticed she hasn't been in school again since half term. Quite a lot of teachers come to Barrow.'

Aha, so most teachers were mental, it was official. The girl's again referred to the time off at the beginning of term because of Phoenix. Penny wondered if she knew about that too. 'Yes,' she said again.

'Really? Which ward is she on? Do you think she'd mind if I popped in to see her?'

She seemed as delighted as Penny would be on being told that Gary Glitter was moving into the house next door. If there'd been a house next door. The bus was turning left onto the hospital road by the big green sign that said Barrow Hospital. Under the sign, a few men in brown coats held a banner with the words OFFICIAL STRIKE, written in clumsy black letters. They weren't making much of an impact at the side of a road with no passing traffic other than an ancient bus carrying two teenage schoolgirls and one nutter (Mr. Cat's-Eyes was on the top deck, she'd seen him as the bus had come round the corner). Perhaps they were waiting to throw rotten eggs at the bosses' cars as they left work for the day. She didn't look too closely in case it turned out JJ was standing there with them, in solidarity, as he would say. 'She's not seeing anyone but family at the moment, but I'll tell her you asked. What's your name?'

'Patricia Cox. Are you coming up on Sunday? That's the main visiting day. There's a bus at two fifteen from the bottom.' She stood up and pulled on the wire to ring the bell. 'Why don't you come and call for me, number twelve, and I'll show you around a bit before you visit your mum.' She turned to get off the bus.

Penny didn't know what else to say so she said yes.

Katherine wasn't waiting in the bus shelter. Penny looked at her watch. A combination of lateness and slowness meant the bus had not arrived until twenty to five. Katherine had probably given up and gone back to the ward. Penny watched the cat-eyed man descend from the top deck and walk towards the path she needed to take. The driver climbed out of his cab and took the opposite path through the woods. She was nervous of walking through the woods on her own, so when two nurses appeared and headed in the right direction she jumped up and followed them, shortening her stride so as not to overtake them.

The nurses at John Cary House said her mother was out at Discussion Group and was not expected to return until five thirty.

'She asked me to bring her this,' said Penny, holding up the bag.

'Oh I see. Was she supposed to meet you? Please don't be upset, your mother's day-to-day memory isn't normal at the moment because of her medication.'

The nurse let her sit in the office while she made a phone call to ask Katherine to come back early and then asked if she minded waiting in the sitting room, which was thankfully empty of people, but noisy with the blare of the radio. Penny pulled a chair closer to the door. Just in case. She put the shirt box on her knees and and used it as a book rest as she pretended to read, her hair falling around her face like a curtain of privacy that she hoped would deter anyone thinking of bothering her while she waited. She had read the same sentence five times over by the time Katherine arrived.

'Hello darling, how nice to see you.'

'Mum, you asked me to come and bring you this.'

'Did I? Well, that's fantastic, thank you.'

'I thought you were going to meet me at the bus stop.'

'Did you? I'm sorry.'

Penny wanted to go home, but she had to wait for the bus. Or else walk, which didn't appeal given that the road home had nothing on either side but woods and orchards. Anyone could have wandered out through the open gates, past the houses and the strikers, and be waiting to pounce on someone like her.

'Let's have some tea,' said Katherine. 'I'm always thirsty these days. It's the tablets. Thank you for my box. How was school?'

They walked through to the kitchen.

'We went on a trip to the Arnolfini and Jackie fainted in front of a mad painting.'

Katherine laughed. 'That doesn't surprise me,' she said. 'Girls your age are always fainting in Assembly at Backwell, usually because they haven't eaten breakfast or because of their periods. It's nothing to worry about. Jackie's just the fainting kind. Unless she's pregnant. Please excuse me a minute, I need to go to the loo. Will you finish making the tea?'

Already, thought Penny, she's got me making the tea. But she did it anyway because it was better than thinking about what Katherine had said about Jackie being pregnant. If Jackie was pregnant, her baby would be Katherine's grandchild; it would be Penny's niece. Aunty Penny. Aunt Penelope. Fuckinell Jack. Fuckinell Phoenix, you moron. What a bloody fucking disaster that would be.

When Katherine came back, Penny said, 'Mum, it's not Dad's fault that Phoenix died.'

'I know.'

***

THE COXES' FRONT GARDEN was two scruffy patches of lawn on either side of a crazy paving path. To one side a long bed was planted with leafless spiky bushes. Their front door was painted the same identical dirty shade of turquoise as the lamp-posts that lined the street, as were all the other front doors in the row, as were all the doors and pipes on the hospital buildings. There was no bell, just a knocker. No sooner had Penny stopped at the door than Patricia appeared at the corner of the house, her Afghan on, ready to go.

Penny thought of the times she'd rung Jackie's unanswered doorbell as arranged, only to discover when they next met that Jackie had been swept up in other plans and forgotten the one made with Penny. Each time Jackie had shrugged off Penny's disappointment with a 'Well, I didn't say for definite.' It had happened so many times that Penny had given up bothering to make arrangements with her outside school unless it was for Jackie to come to her house. That way she was at least saved the long dejected walk home.

'I was watching out for you, because my dad's sleeping,' said Patricia. 'He's on nights. Come on, we'll go the back way.'

Penny wasn't certain what being 'on nights' entailed but if Patricia's father was asleep, she was glad not to have woken him, although she had been hoping for a look inside Patricia's house and maybe to meet her mother.

Patricia led the way around the side of the house, and Penny followed her new friend the length of their back garden, where daffodil spears were growing in random clumps in the long grass and a dark creosoted shed stood alongside a ridged vegetable plot. At the bottom of the garden was an apple tree with an old rope swing hanging from it, under which were strewn the dismembered parts of a motor bike.

'My brother's,' said Patricia. 'It's been there since last summer. Mum's always nagging at him to do something with it, but he's started playing rugby at weekends now, so that's that. He's probably hoping it'll gradually sink into the ground.'

Penny hadn't meant to say anything, but too many links had slotted together in her mind and the words just blurted out of their own accord. 'My dad lives in our shed.'

'Does he? Why?'

Penny imagined the response such a confession of abnormality would elicit from Jackie. 'Well, he works out there anyway, he's a journalist, but since Mum went into the hospital he's stopped coming into the house. At night anyway, I don't know about during the day when I'm at school.'

'You can come and have tea with us then, next time you visit your mum. My mum won't mind, there's always loads. You're not a vegetarian are you? Sean, my brother, is and it drives her mad.'

'Thanks, that's really nice. I'm not a vegetarian,' said Penny. 'My parents used to be, but that was back in the sixties when they did all sorts of weird stuff.'

Patricia laughed. 'Were they hippies? Your mum looks a bit like she used to be a hippy. Like a hippy model. How tall are you?'

'Five feet eleven and a half.'

'You're so lucky. I wish I was that tall.'

Not that Patricia was especially short, about five feet eight, Penny thought, and with her Afghan coat and long unbrushed hair, she didn't look so unlike a hippy model herself.

The girls turned to the right and up a slope towards a group of low brick buildings. The Day Centre, Patricia explained, where ex-patients and outpatients went to work.

'What do they do in there?'

'Make things. I'm not sure. I've never been in there. That bloke who catches the four-fifteen bus, have you noticed him? He goes out to a different day centre in town. We call him Chaser. He used to chase us when we were kids.'

'How come?' Penny attempted to copy Patricia's calm response to abnormal information.

'He thought we liked it. And I suppose we did really, we used to go looking for him. As soon as he ever saw us in the distance, he'd start running, and we'd run away. He'd chase us all the way to the hospital gates.' Patricia laughed at the memory of it.

'What if he'd caught you?'

'He never did. Probably could've easily if he'd wanted to. My friend's dad, they've moved away now, knew him and asked him about it. He said he'd never hurt us and that it was just a bit of fun. And so it was.'

'Haven't you ever spoken to him?' Penny said, recalling they were the only two passengers on the bus every day.

'No,' said Patricia. 'I suppose it's quite funny really.'

It was more scary than funny, but each to their own.

Patricia looked at her watch. 'Right,' she said. 'It's getting on for three, we'd better get a move on.'

Beyond the Day Centre the lane became an unmade track through the woods. They followed it.

'Where are we going?'

'I'll show you.'

The end of the lane joined up with the road that encircled the hospital, and Penny recognized a hexagonal building half-concealed by rhododendron bushes from her walk to the bus stop with JJ.

'That's the morgue,' said Patricia, 'where they put the patients who die without relatives or anyone to give them a proper funeral.'

'That's sad,' said Penny.

Patricia shrugged. 'People die. Some people are disowned by their families when they come here. Others are in and out of here forever until they're too old to leave. Sometimes someone is so depressed or ill that they attempt suicide and get away with it.'

'What do you mean they get away with it? Do they die or don't they?'

'Yes, they kill themselves, but it hardly ever happens. If someone's suicidal, they're watched like a hawk.'

Was Katherine suicidal? It hadn't ever occurred to Penny that her mother might not come home, that she might stay in the hospital until she died, be that sooner or later, naturally or by her own hand. Hadn't Katherine disowned her family instead of the other way around? Perhaps that was a good sign?

They were heading for the hospital gates, but instead of going through them and back towards the houses, they followed the road to the right towards the bus stop where Penny met her mother.

'Why didn't we just walk along the road?' said Penny.

'No reason,' said Patricia. 'Habit I suppose. Smith is on duty at the gatehouse, he's a right grumpy old sod, used to report us when we were kids, so I tend to avoid him when he's there.'

'What did he report you for?'

'Because he hates us. Now he listens in on our phone calls.'

'How can he do that?

'Our phone is linked up to the hospital switchboard, and whoever is on duty at the gatehouse operates the switchboard.'

'Oh,' said Penny. She looked over her shoulder, suddenly insecure in this place where people followed and chased and eavesdropped and told tales. It was enough to send anyone around the bend. 'Do you want to be a nurse?' she said. There was an advertisement for nursing on every second page in *Jackie*.

'No way,' said Patricia. 'I'm going to be an astronomer. What about you?'

'No idea.'

Just before they got to the bus shelter, Patricia pulled at Penny's sleeve and guided her onto the path that Penny had seen the bus driver take.

'What's up here?'

'The nurses' home. And canteen. Fancy some chips?'

'Okay,' said Penny. She'd eaten nothing since breakfast.

They went in by a side door to a narrow corridor with the smell of Sunday roast clinging to its walls.

'Oh, it's Sunday,' said Patricia. 'It'll have to be roast spuds instead. You'll need something solid in your stomach before you see what I'm going to show you. Let's find Rene.'

Rene, pronounced Reenie, was a small woman in a blue-check housecoat with curly bleached hair, freckles and red lipstick, who called Patricia 'my lover'.

Patricia introduced Penny as her new friend.

'She've been cominaround yere on the scrounge since she were a babby,' said Rene, full of pride. 'Youse goin' t'ave summat tweet then?'

'Any spuds left?' said Patricia.

''Course,' said Rene. 'I always makes extra for you. Want some Yorkshires?'

Patricia looked at Penny and Penny smiled. 'Mmm, yes please.'

Rene tutted and rolled her eyes then disappeared through a door behind her. The canteen was empty but for two uniformed nurses sitting in comfy chairs smoking cigarettes, now and then lifting teacups to their lips. They looked too tired to even talk to each other.

Rene returned carrying an oval meat plate stacked high with potatoes and Yorkshire puddings. Penny hadn't bothered to make herself any lunch and her mouth watered at the sight of it.

'Yere you go, youse can share a plate to save on the old washing-up.'

Patricia bowed her head close to Rene's ear and at first Penny thought she was going to kiss the woman on the cheek, but instead she whispered something. Rene shook her head as if in disappointment. 'I'll give you the key when you'm finished eating,' she said, and turned back into the kitchen.

They ate with their fingers, wiping them from time to time on white paper serviettes pulled from a dispenser next to the cutlery stand. Penny didn't know Patricia well enough to ask what the whispering was about, but assumed it must be connected with the thing that required a full stomach.

The potatoes were overcooked and wrinkled and the Yorkshires were soggy from sitting around, but it was the most delicious meal she had tasted in weeks, not least because it had been prepared by someone other than herself and wasn't made of fish, chips, beans or toast. Penny slumped back in her chair, hands resting on her stomach.

'If you've had enough, we'd better get on with it or you won't have time to see your mum,' said Patricia.

They hadn't made much of a dent in the mountain on the plate, and Patricia's face feigned regret as she handed the remains back through the serving hatch.

'I've opened up,' said Rene. 'Youse can go on round.'

Patricia beamed at her, turned to Penny and flicked her head towards the door. She led the way down the corridor to another door marked Kitchen Staff Only. Patricia looked left and right, then pushed it open, waved Penny in and quickly closed it behind them. They were in a small bright room that smelled of cleaning materials. Light came in through a long horizontal window of dimpled glass and with bars on the outside. Shelves ran the length of the wall below it, stacked with giant tins of coffee, pickled onions and eggs, Branston pickle and other tinned food at one end, and giant packets of paper serviettes, folded overalls and tin foil at the other. An industrial food mixer sat on top of a filing cabinet with metal serving trays of all shapes and sizes propped behind its.

It was hard to see what the excitement was about, but when she looked around Patricia had climbed up on a step stool and was reaching something down from the furthest corner of the top shelf, so she guessed she was about to find out.

'Before they built the canteen, this used to be a teaching room,' she said. 'No one else knows about this but Rene and me.' In her two hands, she was holding a jar larger than any of the pickle jars, filled with something that looked at a distance like vinegar. Floating in it was an object that Penny was unable to make out properly until Patricia returned to ground level and placed the jar on the counter.

'Come and see,' she said.

Penny leaned in for a closer look then jumped quickly back when she identified the contents of the jar. 'Yuck,' she said, her face burning with embarrassment.

Patricia laughed. 'What do you mean? Don't you think it's beautiful?'

Floating in the jar, like a giant pickled egg, was a foetus. 'Whose is it?'

Patricia shrugged. 'Dunno, probably been here for donkey's years. Rene found it six years ago when she was given the room to use as a store cupboard. It must have been used for teaching. Who knows?'

'Even so, it must have come from somewhere,' said

Penny. 'From someone.' She moved in again for a closer look. It was more than a foetus. It was a fully developed human baby and Penny couldn't stop herself thinking about Jackie and the thing that might be growing inside her, planted there by Phoenix.

'Look at its little willy,' said Patricia, planting a finger on the jar. 'Look how dinky it is.'

'Oh god,' said Penny, partly because the song "Little Willy" by Sweet had started up at the back of her mind.

'My mum told me,' said Patricia, 'that not so long ago, if a female patient got pregnant, especially if it was by another patient, the doctors would sometimes abort the baby without the mother's permission. This poor thing was probably the result of desperate shag in the woods by two patients.'

'Or a rape,' said Penny. 'Perhaps a girl got raped and went mad afterwards and had to come here, then discovered she was pregnant and the doctors got rid of it for her.'

Patricia shrugged and nodded at the possibility.

Surely it wasn't hygienic to keep that thing in there with the food? The smell of cleaning fluid was making Penny feel sick despite, or perhaps because of, the number of potatoes she had eaten. Either way, she needed to get some fresh air. 'I feel a bit sick,' she said.

'Oh, sorry,' said Patricia. 'Why don't you go and wait outside while I put this away.'

Outside, Penny gulped down the damp air and felt instantly better, as long as she averted her gaze from the catkins, which dangled from the hazel behind her and bore too close a resemblance to the tiny pickled penis to be anything other than disturbing.

Patricia apologized for having left her alone for so long - she'd had to lock up and return the key to Rene - but not for having scared her half to death. Patricia had the air of having never been scared by anything; she read books about aliens and mad things that would happen in the future.

'Is your mum on one of the villas? I'll walk you over there.'

Penny hoped she wasn't going to expect to come in and see Katherine in an 'I'll show you mine if' kind of way.

'She's in John Cary House,' said Penny, unsure even if it was all right to reveal that kind of information without first asking her mother. But Katherine was away with the fairies; Penny had to make her own decisions now.

'Really? My mum works on the ward next door. Combe. John Cary and Combe are always competing. My ward's cleaner than your ward, and all that. But John Cary is the poshest villa. It's run by Monty Wild and he insists they have comfy chairs and nice curtains like at home. My mum worked on there for a bit, she says it's the best ward to work on at Barrow, so it's probably the best ward to be on as a patient.'

They followed Penny's usual route to John Cary House. Patricia pointed out the ward where her dad worked and the ward where Chaser lived, but otherwise they walked in silence.

When they emerged onto the road, Patricia stopped and said she would leave Penny there because she was going back the way they had come and said that if Penny was coming again tomorrow she could come for tea at her house at six o'clock. Either she could give her a backy home on her bike, or her brother could drive her if he was home.

***

JJ SPENT THE LAST FEW DAYS OF THE ELECTION campaign in the central library, researching and making notes until chucking-out time at eight. From there he made his way to sparsely-attended candlelit meetings in draughty halls on dark streets. It took no more than five of those days to convince him that unless someone did something drastic, Labour was on course to lose, at least in Bristol. JJ was in the mood for doing something drastic. Armed with a torch, a flask of tomato soup and a bagful of leaflets and posters taken from one of Tony Benn's public meetings in Southmead, he took it upon himself to walk the streets of that foreign constituency, all night if he had to, knocking on doors, a persuasive rant composed and committed to memory. The night was another foggy one and he was alone. Normal people canvassed in daylight, but JJ was on a mission.

So far people had been polite, especially those who had already decided to spend their vote elsewhere, their voices filled with pity at the sight of that poor man sent out on such an obvious lost cause. One woman with a sky-blue poster in her front window - JJ had shone his torch on it to check before knocking - had even invited him in for tea and biscuits. It was only after he'd knocked at her next-door neighbour's house with its red poster and therefore presumably Labour allegiance that he wished he'd taken her up on her offer.

'Clear off before I bite your head off.'

Convinced that the red-faced man had been expecting someone else and would be glad of a few moments to regain his composure, JJ launched into his prepared introduction. But he was wrong.

'I know who you are, you're that bleeding idiot from the Post. Now clear off out of here or I'll rip my poster down, roll it up and shove it up your backside.' He followed up on his threat by opening his mouth wide, and snapping his teeth together while making a snarling sound in the back of his throat.

At the sound of rattling phlegm, JJ took a step backwards. Message received. 'Er, I'm sure Mr Wedgwood-Benn will appreciate your voting for him despite any, er, personal grievance you may hold against me,' said JJ as he walked backwards down the path, which sloped at such a subtle angle that it almost toppled him in his retreat.

'Bugger off,' came the response.

JJ turned and walked away as fast as he could without seeming terrified. The door slammed behind him. He moved off down the street, missing out a few houses to ensure a safe distance before starting again. It irked him to have incited such ire in a fellow Labour supporter; he had never been attacked with such bile before, not even in his own home. It must have been something he'd written. He checked his watch; a quarter to ten, people would soon be going to bed.

He resumed his rounds. The party political broadcast that night was from the Liberal party, so he intended to continue knocking on doors while it was on, but from ten fifteen onwards it would be enough just to feed leaflets and posters through letterboxes, he didn't want to be talking to women in quilted dressing gowns and curlers in their hair on the doorstep. Nor did he want to be rousing people from their beds; he had incurred enough wrath for one night. All he could do was his best, he had been told as a child, even if his best didn't match up to his vision of his own potential; this was the very reasoning he held responsible for the lack of achievement in his life so far, but for once he was comforted by it. It was his saving grace, his safety net. He'd be all right.

He sat down at a bus stop and poured a cup of soup from his flask. The street smelled of woodsmoke. Most of the houses here would be without central heating, their inhabitants waking up with ice on the inside of their windows like he had in the shed that very morning. No wonder they were cross.

The ability to provoke a strong reaction was an achievement in its own right, he supposed, he only wished he knew how he'd done it so that next time it could be tailored to inspire the wrath of those on the opposite side of the political fence. He decided to go back and find out.

It was ten to eleven. The early shutdown had been called off for the election and the grey light of the television could be seen still flickering in the gap between the man's curtains. Without pausing to think about what he was going to say, JJ lifted the metal bar at the base of the letterbox and let it drop. Twice. He heard the heavy thud of footsteps on the other side of the door; it had failed to enter his consciousness on his last visit to this address that its resident was a big bloke, but it struck him now, too late.

'Thought I told you to clear off.'

'Yes, you did, and I'm sorry to disturb you again, but I'd really like to know what I've done to offend you.'

The man took a step backwards as if JJ had raised a nailed club against him, his eyes widened with an emotion that, if you hadn't witnessed his earlier belligerence, you might interpret as fear. JJ wasn't so stupid as to allow himself such an obvious mistake and took a step backwards himself in case his opponent was planning to take a running jump at him. But the man had stopped snarling, his accent melted to a warm burr.

'You're a hypocrite,' he said. 'You all are.'

'I'm sorry,' said JJ. 'I don't understand.'

'Hypocrite. Someone what says one thing and does summat different.'

'I know what the word means,' said JJ. 'I don't

understand what, specifically, you are referring to.' He shuffled his feet in an unenthusiastic flamenco, they were numb from standing around in the freezing fog, and while JJ didn't know why he had adopted the tone of a grammar school headmaster addressing some wayward scholarship oik, he was happy to see it had had some effect.

'Better come in,' said the man.

JJ's reticence to enter stemmed from a reluctance to reach thawing out point only to have to go back outside and acclimatize all over again, or so he told himself. But he needn't have worried because the man seemed to have calmed down and the front room was also freezing but for the few feet in front of a two-bar electric heater. A winged armchair, the seat of which had been bagged by an obese tabby, was soaking up the lion's share of the heat.

The man dragged a dining chair into the room and set it down next to the armchair, then he shooed the cat away and sat down, gesturing to JJ to take the hard chair. JJ was surprised to note that the man had chosen to avoid all the late-night political programmes and was tuned instead to what appeared to be a ballroom dancing competition. And on top of that he seemed to have forgotten why JJ was in his house.

'So,' said JJ, attempting to jog his memory, and he needed to say no more.

'I works on the railways, down at Temple Meads,' the man stretched his hands out towards the heater. 'I reads

193

your column every week, sometimes it's quite good, I'll give you that, but you journalists thinks you'm above it all.'

The sparse furnishings - the two chairs, a low-slung oak coffee table, a walnut sideboard and a brass poker lying redundant in the brown tiled hearth - symbolized the home of a lonely man who thinks too much, thought JJ. The man had stopped talking and JJ was none the wiser as to his captor's accusations. At his feet, JJ's bag bulged accusingly with unposted leaflets. He opened his mouth to say something that might speed things up, but the man started up again.

'It gets my gall,' he said.

'What does?'

'You lot,' said the man. 'Everyone's behind them miners. Every single bugger supported the proposal except the bloody NUJ. And where was your column that week? No-bloody-where, that's where. We was all waiting to see what you had to say about it, I even wrote in to the Post but of course they never printed it. 'S'all right to criticize other people's ways but when it comes to you and your crew you just disappears. Cowards, that's what you'm are.'

Every word of his speech was delivered to the heater; not once did the man even glance at JJ. He gave the impression of having made his case so many times to nobody listening that when at last a real-life audience turned up he could only communicate by pretending they weren't there.

And the foundry workers, JJ wanted to say. And the foundry workers. They hadn't supported the strike proposal either. But the accusation was less about the lack of support than about JJ's failure to comment upon it, to condemn it publicly and effectively self-criticize. The foundry-working membership didn't, as far as JJ was aware, write newspaper columns. But JJ was getting off the point. At least he knew now what his crime was. The TUC had proposed to the government that if the miners' pay claim could be awarded as a special case, the other unions would agree not to claim for exceptional circumstances in the future thereby avoiding a precedent dangerous to the government. All the unions, with the exception of the foundry workers and the NUJ, had supported the proposal at a special conference on the sixteenth of January, the day after Phoenix's funeral. In the end, the proposal had gone nowhere, but JJ could recall the day in question clearly: the scene of three shell-shocked people in dressing gowns clearing up after a party that had varied so drastically from the one held in the same place just a couple of weeks before because it was a wake. They hadn't known what else to do with the rest of that day, so they had gone to the grave and stood in the sunshine by the frost-covered mound of red earth, beside the wilting roses and lilies and read the accompanying sympathy messages.

They'd been lucky to get a family plot; JJ and Katherine hadn't even considered making plans for their own deaths; if they were too young, what did that make Phoenix?

If he told the man all this, he could be accused of going

for the sympathy vote, you couldn't expect a stranger, a man with no family life of his own, who seemed to have nothing at all in his life besides his work, to understand that at that time nothing was further from JJ's mind than a union ballot.

He knew that what he was about to say would render him even more of a pillock in the man's eyes than he doubtless already was, but he could live with that; to roll out the death-in-the-family excuse was unthinkable.

'I was abroad that week,' said JJ. 'At a friend's wedding in France. I'm sorry.'

The man shook his head, and kept on shaking it, speechless, unable to express the extent of his disappointment. JJ knew he had lost a valuable reader. In letting this one man down he may as well have alienated his whole readership, for this man was a valid representative of the whole. What JJ didn't know was that as he'd been speaking tears had spilled onto his numb cheeks and dried there, evaporated by the heat of the fire.

'Well, I'd best be off if I'm to get rid of all these leaflets tonight,' said JJ.

The man levered himself out of his chair. 'I'll give you a hand,' he said. 'Wait while I get my coat.'

JJ stood up to protest, but the man had already left the room. He trailed after him into the hallway where the man handed him a shopping bag from the under-stairs cupboard. 'Yere,' he said. 'Chuck some o'they leaflets in that.' As he shut the garden gate behind them he told

JJ that his street would be a waste of time. 'Bunch of working-class Tory bastards,' he said. 'They'd vote for Hitler if he came back tomorrow.'

'Maybe Enoch Powell should be making a leadership bid then,' said JJ as they set off down the street.

The man harrumphed.

'I'm sorry,' said JJ. 'I don't know your name.'

'Tony,' said the man. 'Tony Benson.'

'No!' said JJ. 'Is it really?'

''Fraid so,' said Tony, shaking his head. 'The number of times I've been asked if that's why I vote Labour. Shows how stupid people are.'

When Enoch Powell declared his support for Labour two days later JJ considered a special trip back to see Tony in Southmead, but his desperation to share the news with another human only underlined the painful truth that he was sitting alone in his shed listening to the radio instead of in his own sitting room, with the woman he loved, watching historic events unfold on the telly and taking full aphrodisiac advantage of the ensuing debate.

Should Labour welcome the fascist vote? His answer of course was a resounding negative, even though he knew that to split the right-wing vote was perhaps the only chance Labour had of winning.

JJ hadn't seen Penny for days, but the lights in the house had been going on and off at regular intervals, so he assumed she was all right and was spending time up at the hospital with Katherine. Children adjusted so much more easily to life's fluctuations. He picked at his beard. Claustrophobia was becoming a problem. The shed seemed to be shrinking the more time he spent in it. Canvassing offered an escape of sorts, but was really little more than an extension of his daily walk, and besides, if you are out walking in smog you may as well be in a cardboard box. For so long he had fantasized about a solitary writing life. Now it had become his reality, he missed his real life.

Peering out of his window at the unlit kitchen, he wondered where they had all gone, the people who had lived in that house. Where was the endless stream of teenagers and Gingerbread unmarried mothers who would let themselves in at the back door without stopping to knock? Of course they had never been there to see him, were indeed the reason he had taken to working in the shed in the first place, but he missed them. It struck him how few people he knew, how little effort he had put into friendships.

There he was, in a shed, in the garden of a house, which was a quarter of a mile from its nearest neighbour and a mile from the village that provided the second to last line of its postal address. That village was five miles from the city centre, which in turn was one hundred and twenty-something miles from the capital. At that point in time and space, John Jacobs was a very small man indeed.

The doctor had insisted that Katherine was making

good progress, whatever that meant. That she had befriended a teenage anorexic was seen as a positive sign; patients were encouraged to help one other. To JJ's ears that seemed less like progress and more like Katherine doing the same in hospital as she would be doing in her free time at home, so did nothing to explain why she still needed to be there. And how could it be progress when she still refused to see him? When had everyday life become so much more difficult to understand than politics?

At least Penny would be fine, she'd been in a permanent state of mortification at her family's behaviour for years, nothing they did now could make it any worse for her. She had Jackie and her Saturday job and her pop stars and the one thing that he wanted, which was access to Katherine. He had no one, not one person to confide in, not his parents who knew nothing of his current predicament, not his boss, not the woman he loved. Even the cats seemed to have deserted the place, and the robin was increasingly casual about showing up for breakfast.

It was for this reason that JJ had distanced himself from his daughter: he didn't want to be one of those parents dependent on their child for emotional succour, or one who grilled them for information about a divorced other half, if it should come to that. But in lieu of that contact, his life ticked by as a shallow grey pulse persists in the wrist of a dying man.

He stopped picking at his beard, as if an invisible hand had slapped his away from his face in a stroke of pull-yourself-together admonishment and he put his beard-picking hand to better use and picked up his pen. He had already written and filed his response to a Tory victory, and was midway through the Labour version. He read back what he had written so far:

> *Let this be a lesson for us, and for our children: the voters of the future. Let us always remember this period as a benchmark for what we can and must achieve if we find ourselves encumbered by a Prime Minister with the moral compass of a paedophile priest, or a Home Secretary with the scruples of Himmler. When we next find ourselves at the mercy of government propaganda that abuses words like 'freedom' and 'democracy', uses them to justify a suspect cause, like Hitler did and Franco did and Johnson did and Kruschev did, and the CIA did in Chile last September, we know what to do. We have to watch these people like hawks and we have to bring them down.*

A bit melodramatic, but what the hell; Labour hads as much chance of winning as the Pope had of sleeping with Liz Taylor.

***

OVER TEA LOUISA SUGGESTED THEY GO TO a drama group that evening run by a group of volunteers called Toc H. Drama group wasn't the most popular activity on offer, being timetabled at the end of the week when most people were worn out from a week of occupational therapy, working on the farm, or just wandering about; most people preferred to stay in and watch television and it was the attraction of a sparsely-populated room that enabled Louisa to persuade Katherine to go with her.

Other Catherine was in the telephone box outside Combe Villa as they passed, ringing for a taxi to come and take her home the next day.

'The nurses don't bother to stop her anymore,' said Louisa. 'The taxi company know her now so they never send a car, but they stay on the phone to her for ages. I think she just rings them for a chat. Rather them than me.'

Katherine wasn't really listening. That morning, as every morning, a letter had arrived for Katherine, addressed in JJ's spidery hand. She had progressed to the point where she could take the letter from the nurse and hold it for a few seconds without tearing it into pieces, before handing it back. The nurse tucked it under her arm while she handed out any other mail, then took it to be locked away with the steadily accumulating pile of identical others.

Drama group was held in the recreation hall, which on Sunday mornings served as a chapel where staff and patients could attend mass together, and at other times hosted all kinds of social events: film shows, beetle drives, bingo, staff dances. Louisa had told her that every Christmas a staff amateur theatre company staged a pantomime for the patients; last Christmas they had performed Babes in the Wood, with real children playing the babes. Louisa thought they were the children of staff who lived up at the staff houses.

It was more of a large Nissen hut, more temporary-seeming than the word 'hall' implied. It had a pointed roof and five windows along each side. A hand-drawn poster in a plastic bag, advertising a forthcoming beetle drive, was fixed to the outer door with drawing pins.

Inside it smelled of wood and polish, with a subliminal whiff of spilled beer. Its stage was end-on with red velvet curtains pulled across it. To one side, in a recess, was a bar area kept safe from pilfering hands by a metal grille. Chairs and folding tables were stacked along one side of the room. High up on the walls, in the spaces between the windows, electric bar heaters shed their orange glow downwards: three on each side plus one above the entrance and another above the bar, all operated by the pull of a cord, their output insufficient to heat the room.

For the first time since they had met, Louisa was not carrying her notebook, and when Katherine asked where her play was, it happened to be within earshot of one of the Toc H people, Maria. A mistake that backfired on her immediately.

'Are you writing a play, Louisa?' said Maria.

'No,' said Louisa. 'But Katherine is, she's a drama teacher.'

She hadn't told anyone but Louisa that she was a drama teacher, because she wasn't one in the hospital, and in all likelihood she wouldn't be one when she came out. But Louisa told Maria now, in a fit of spontaneous deflection, who thought it was fabulous, even if Katherine had corrected the statement with a 'used to be'. Maria invited her to lead the class one evening if she felt so inclined. Katherine shook her head, panic rising in her throat at the very idea.

They began the class with simple physical exercises to get their circulation going, and as they stood in a circle of nine and jumped up and down, their breath puffed up above their heads like empty speech bubbles.

While for the other members of the group, the act of jumping involved little more than lifting both heels off the floor at more or less the same time, Louisa jumped with her whole body, bringing her knees right up to her chest like a footballer warming up on the touchline. It was exhausting to watch, and when it elicited a mild 'Don't overdo it, Louisa' from one of the group leaders it dawned on Katherine that this was another symptom of her anorexia and that she relished drama group as a legitimate arena for vigorous exercise, which was otherwise restricted to the practice of press-ups and sit-ups in the fifteen-minute breaks between night-time checks, and only then when she could get away with not taking her Mogadon.

After the warm up the class consisted for the most part of improvisation exercises, with rounds of applause at the end of each one. Katherine preferred to watch rather than join in, promising to participate more the following week.

As she helped to stack chairs at the end of the class, Maria asked Katherine in a soft voice if she would be interested in bringing her play along to show her, because if she were Maria would love to see it. Katherine promised to think about it.

The walk back to John Cary House was short but pretty, taking them as it did through intermittent pools of soft orange light cast down by the street lamps. Louisa rabbited on, but Katherine was too tired to listen and could only wonder at the source of Louisa's inexhaustible energy. She decided the girl was surviving thanks only to a cocktail of youth and adrenaline.

Back on the ward, people were watching *Within These Walls*. Even Gordon had raised his head from his hands. They had missed the eight o'clock drug round so Katherine collected her amitriptyline from the nurse and made her own Horlicks to wash it down. Unable to face the sitting room she took what had become her usual seat in the dining room. She folded her arms on the cool formica, lowered her head onto her arms, and waited for tears.

There was nothing unusual in that place about sitting for hours with tears soaking into your sleeves. Katherine was not the first to do it – she had even seen staff come close to it - and she would not be the last. People came and went around her, in and out of the kitchen, running errands, chatting, filling cups and glasses. Some she heard, some she didn't. When at last the tears came they were not accompanied by the loud noisy sobs that had leapt from her at her son's funeral, but were as constant as the trickle of the overflow that relieves a full bath.

At ten the nurse brought her Mogadon. Katherine refused; if she couldn't be present at the end for her own son then the least she could do was to be awake to experience her own demise. But she must have fallen asleep anyway, because when she next raised her head, the television in the sitting room had been switched off and the dining room was in darkness but for an elongated rectangle of light from the kitchen that lit the floor. A glass of water had been placed next to her on the table and Katherine gulped it down. Her throat was tight; her head ached and her belly was empty; and the muscles in her arms and legs wouldn't move even if she wanted them to. She let out a protracted sigh that died out with a shudder.

The sound of rubber soles peeling off sticky lino crept up behind her, then a warm hand on her back and a soft male voice. 'Would you like some warm milk?' The voice moved in closer to whisper in her ear. 'I'm sure the Colonel wouldn't mind if we put a nip of brandy in it.'

Katherine nodded and the nurse retreated. The Colonel, who had witnessed who knew what horrors in both world wars and had become so entrenched in his memories that he found himself unable to function out of uniform, had in 1968 swallowed the little capsule of cyanide that he'd been given in 1939. But the pill had lost its potency, his attempt to shut out the chaos failed and the Colonel had ended up in Barrow. A man once responsible for the lives of thousands could no longer be trusted with his own. Brandy was his life's only remaining pleasure and every evening at eight o'clock he was allowed a tipple to wash his pills down; at all other times the bottle was locked for safekeeping in the office. No one gets off scot-free, she thought, we all suffer, even the apparently successful and privileged. What would JJ make of that?

The nurse - Katherine didn't even know which nurse it was, her eyes were too sore to keep them open for long - brought the warm milk and sat down beside her, placing a light hand on her forearm. So he had seen those films too, where people were brought back from the brink of death by the power of a loved one holding their hand and praying. If only Katherine could have had the chance to do that for Phoenix, things would be so different. She lowered her head again and the milk went cold.

She was woken in the night by screaming. It stopped when she opened her eyes so at first she mistook it for the echo of a bad dream; but within seconds it started up again. She kicked her legs free of the blankets and sat up to listen.

Outside in the corridor, the rush of feet and the opening and closing of a door.

Katherine's hand folded over the cold brass doorknob and turned it to the right. If anyone saw her she would say she needed the loo. A strip of light under Louisa's door confirmed her suspicions as to the source of the commotion. She knew Louisa had planned to avoid taking her moggies that night, she had been boasting about a new technique that involved rolling the pill from side to side under her tongue as the nurse checked her mouth. Katherine had grown accustomed to Louisa's wiliness, but she was very sick, and now she was in trouble.

The screaming subsided, and Katherine took a few steps out into the corridor and understood for the first time where she was. In a psychiatric hospital, in the company of people far sicker than herself, and she was not one of the staff; she was one of them, one of the loonies.

From behind Louisa's door came sounds of great gulping sobs and the calming tones of the nurse. Katherine dropped her chin and watched her own feet progress along the red carpet; a bad colour for a carpet, she thought again, the colour of dried blood, shows everything. Except dried blood.

The Welsh nurse appeared at the top of the stairs. 'Don't worry,' she said to Katherine. 'She's all right, she's been exercising again. You go back to bed.'

Katherine pointed towards the toilets.

'Okay,' the nurse nodded. 'Then go back to sleep, it's

only four o'clock. Are you all right?'

Katherine nodded and continued on her way even though the desire to pee had subsided.

The reflection of the overhead light off the glossed walls made her squint. The change from carpet to linoleum chilled her feet. She lifted her nightie and sat down on the cold hard toilet seat, pressing her left foot down onto her right so that at least one of them might be warm. She was thirsty again, always thirsty. She leaned forward, elbows on knees, head in hands, and the sleeves of her nightie slipped down to expose her goose-bumped skin, and as the thin stream of urine trickled into the porcelain bowl, so did two mercurial streams escape from the corners of her eyes, roll down her forearms and soak into the winceyette cuffs of her nightie.

Then someone was knocking at the door.

'Katherine, are you in there? Open the door please.'

A male voice. JJ? The knocking sharpened.

'Katherine, I'm going to open the door myself.'

He could do it; anyone could do it, the old school trick, you simply pressed a finger against the word *engaged* and pushed the dial in the right direction until *vacant* appeared in its place. Katherine dithered, confused. Why was she locked in the toilet? She tried to speak out but her mouth was gummed up, her tongue stuck to the roof of her mouth. By the time it had loosened and released the knob on her side of the door had moved around and the door inched open towards her toes. The red head and white shoulder of the male nurse wedged themselves between wall and door. 'Did you fall asleep?'

Katherine shrugged.

'I'll wait outside and help you back to your room.' He retreated and Katherine heard him whisper to someone out in the corridor. She pulled a couple of sheets of toilet paper from their letterbox dispenser and threw them straight into the toilet, another school trick, then reached a slow hand up to pull on the metal stirrup that hung from the end of the toilet chain.

The red-haired nurse smiled as he linked Katherine's arm through his own. She stood a head taller than him but his grip was strong and the physical contact was a comfort.

'Come on, you must be frozen.'

The warmth of the rough carpet was welcome under her toes. Had she dreamed the commotion earlier? Louisa's door was shut and in darkness. 'Sorry,' she said.

'No need to apologize. There's always fun and games on the full moon.'

That confirmed it for her; she had been demoted to the rank of fully-fledged lunatic.

She woke again as people were making their way down to breakfast; she quickly dressed and joined them. Louisa was seated at their table, paler and thinner than ever. Other Catherine was helping to serve breakfast. Katherine held out her plate for the usual scrambled egg and tomato.

'Are you sure that's all you want?' said Catherine. 'You look tired, dear. Why don't you put on a bit of make-up to cheer yourself up?'

Katherine was too exhausted to raise a smile of condescension. Catherine leaned in closer and the alcohol stench of freshly sprayed perfume was suffocating.

'I'm going home today, dear,' she said.

'No you are not,' said Katherine.

'Yes, dear, that's right. That's what they tell the others, so no one gets upset.'

Katherine collected her cutlery and made for the table where Louisa was engaged in her agonizing cutting and shuffling rituals.

'They're moving me,' Louisa said.

'What do you mean?'

'Back onto the locked ward. Twenty-four hour supervision. They say I'm not eating, telltale bitches. They're making it up. I've told them you see me eat every mealtime but they don't believe me and I bet they haven't even asked you. Anyone can see I'm getting fat. Anyone would get fat in here the amount of food they stuff down you, and nothing to do. It's worse than school. At least there we had to exercise. They hate me here and my parents love it because it's free. They'll force-feed me, you know, they won't be happy until I'm so fat I explode.'

'I'll miss you,' said Katherine. 'I'll come and visit you.'

'They won't let you.'

'When I get out they will.'

'They won't.'

They continued their disagreement in silence.

For the first time since they had shared a table, Louisa was allowed to leave it without proving she had eaten a certain percentage of her food, and was taken off to pack. They'd given up on her, she was someone else's problem from now on. Katherine stayed behind to finish her tea.

StephanieSalome had stopped dancing. Katherine watched her take her place in the breakfast queue. The smile on her face had been wiped away by the drag of a pharmaceutical veil, her eighth veil. With her alter ego suppressed and reintegrated, if she responded at all it was to the name Stephanie. It was as if the usual process of a woman's life, the gradual evolution from freedom to entrapment, whose advance was in general so slow as to be imperceptible, in Stephanie had been time-lapsed into a forty-eight hour period.

Katherine had convinced herself over the years that by avoiding marriage she could cheat that creeping diminishment, but now she recognized that reasoning for what it was, a placebo, a placebo to suck on while the metamorphosis happened anyway. There were no rules. For all Katherine knew her process might have been completed years before she even met JJ. Release was in its reversal. StephanieSalome had stopped dancing, and

Louisa had gone and Katherine was her own jailer.

Gazing out at the grey, late February morning, the events of the night before replayed in her mind. Louisa had been caught and that was all. It was easy to believe you were being left to your own devices, but they were watching you, of course they were, and if you started to behave out of the ordinary - talking about going home was ordinary for Catherine, dancing was, or used to be, ordinary for Stephanie, shitting and jigging was ordinary for Iris, poor soul - they were on to you. Louisa's behaviour was ordinary for her but she supposed it had become insupportable.

What was ordinary for her, Katherine? A routine modified to such a minute degree from the one at home that the differences were noticeable only by inspecting the details of it: get up, have breakfast, spend the day in an institution surrounded by her peers, many of whom she knew found it difficult to function in the world outside, go home again, eat dinner, watch television, go to bed. The template was the same, and wherever she went it would be the same, because wherever she went she would make it the same. From day to day it was the people, the conversations, the variations in detail that fooled you into thinking the template was a shifting malleable structure but really it was fixed and rigid as the artificial Christmas tree that was dragged down from the loft year after year to be decorated with the tinsel and baubles that diverted your attention away from the predictability of it all.

Katherine placed Louisa's still-full plate on top of her own empty one for the last time and picked them up. Iris gurgled at her from her chair as she passed.

'Good morning, Iris,' she said, and patted her arm. We're the same, you and me, she thought, no control, no power. All we can do is observe and depend on the kindness of others.

Louisa left without saying goodbye, but that night when Katherine slid between cold sheets, her knees came to rest upon something flat and hard. She reached down into the bed and dragged an object the size of a thick rectangular place mat into the dim light of the bedside lamp. Louisa's book. It had been instilled into her so often that its contents were private, nay, sacred territory, that she could not bring herself to open it; its transferral to her safekeeping was by no means to be misconstrued as an invitation to explore the secret ramblings of an anorexic mind, but rather a desperate attempt to protect its secrets.

But the next morning, as she lifted the book into the sliver of silver light that divided the curtains, she changed her mind, switched on the lamp and opened it at the first page. Instead of the opening scenes of a play, or the list of characters that you would expect to find in a notebook dedicated to the art of playwriting, the first two pages contained a list of foods with their calorific values listed alongside. Every other page, under date headings, showed endless calculations, scattered in huddles that disregarded the lines on the paper, like collections of insects or chromosomes, some crossed out, others, the daily totals, highlighted in rough-drawn cubes.

Katherine puzzled for a moment over the reality of calculating the calorific value of a quarter of a pea, and the sort of mind that might be compelled to make the effort, then closed the book and, for want of anything better to do with it, shoved it back under the covers where she had found it, switched off the light and got out of bed to open the curtains.

A young blonde woman with reddened eyes and a face destroyed by misery, who had smothered her baby daughter, moved into Louisa's room. Meal times were quieter.

Seasons In The Sun

PENNY DREW HER KNEES, STICKY WITH COOL TAN lotion, in towards her chest to bring her whole body into the shade of the straw umbrella. It was their sixth day in Torremolinos, and while Penny's near-translucent skin was tinted a pale shade of pink when she inspected it through the lenses of her heart-shaped sunglasses, she knew that if she lay down on the sand she would disappear, camouflaged like a sand lizard. *The Female Eunuch* lay at her feet, its pages dotted with greasy fingerprints, its covers curling in the heat.

Jackie was stretched out next to her on a parallel sun lounger, sweat glistening on her already tanned back and legs. Penny stared, as she had numerous times in the weeks leading up to their holiday when she'd thought Jackie wasn't looking, at her friend's midriff, looking for signs of a tightening waistband or stretching skin. She was too scared to confront Jackie outright about the possibility of her being pregnant because, despite hours of searching through back issues of Cathy and Claire, she had still not worked out how she would react to the news, should it be true. It was three months since the evil coupling and Jackie's stomach was as flat as ever so Penny was relaxing into the opinion that Katherine's statement had been no more than a blot on the landscape during the vague meanderings of an addled mind, even if events were suggesting otherwise.

On the horizon, two shades of blue met in a dead straight line, and Penny shifted her thoughts to dwell on how distance could smooth out the waves and, as if it was an inevitable byproduct of that thought, experienced a twinge of homesickness. By looking out to sea she could pretend that their beach formed the fringe of a sub-standard paradise, but there were four things about this holiday that she hadn't anticipated and that she only had to turn her head to either side or look behind her to remember:

(1) Torremolinos was a building site;

(2) It was too hot;

(3) All the men were short;

(4) Jackie was boring;

(5) Five things. She was homesick; not for the home she left behind five days ago, but the one she had before Phoenix died. And not only was Jackie boring but stupid as well and the reason they were facing different directions now was because they had had a row. Jackie's mum had told Jackie to stay out of the sun today because she had been sick after last night's dinner (a huge plate of paella

that they had all shared so it couldn't be food poisoning). Jackie's mum suspected nothing more harmful than sunstroke. Anyway, when Penny reminded Jackie of her promise to her mother, Jackie had told her to mind her own business and thrown a huge sulk. Actually it was Penny's business for two reasons: one, because the luxury of having a private bathroom in their room was being ruined by the stink of vomit and two, if she was going to have a kid, Penny didn't want her baby niece or nephew to be born shrivelled from too much sun.

There had been fun on the holiday though. Penny had never flown before and the flight over in a pink-and-orange plane had been fun. She'd half-expected to see Phoenix sitting out there cross-legged on the thick wad of cloud with his long hair all golden and a pair of wings stuck to his back. She'd refrained from mentioning this to Jackie.

At the end of each term the nuns returned all confiscated items and this term Jackie had been the recipient of a long-forgotten magazine, which she had saved for the journey because it featured an interview with Marc Bolan accompanied by a full-page photograph. Looking not unlike a Spanish waiter on his day off, Marc was dressed in a red-and-white wide-striped silk bomber jacket, unzipped to the waist, and white silk Oxford bags with, and this had been the cause of much excitement and giggling – and possibly the original confiscation, but neither of them could remember - no underpants. The outline of his willy was clearly to be seen curled up like a little hamster at the top of his left trouser leg, and from the look on his face he knew exactly what the girls were looking at.

'Naughty Marc,' Jackie had whispered. 'If you can see it that clearly when it's soft, imagine what it'd be like when he's got a hard-on.'

They had imagined all the way to Malaga, gorging on so much free fizzy that Jackie got travel-sick on the bus from the airport to Torremolinos and had to throw up into a paper bag.

And dinner the first night had been fun. Penny enjoyed listening to people complain about the bread because she'd had a baguette before and knew it wasn't stale, and watching the woman at the next table trying to spread olive oil onto her bread with her knife. Rooting for Jackie's dad at the Mastermind contest started off being fun too, but when he proved to be a bit lacking on the general knowledge front it made Penny homesick for her more intelligent parents. She wondered if either of them had noticed her absence yet.

Besides lying on the beach or at the poolside, they'd spent the first few days looking around the town, where they'd watched American soldiers playing tag at an outdoor café and followed a couple of German boys as far as a hotel at the other end of the town.

Then boredom set in. Until, on day four, Jackie spotted a waiter she fancied in one of the beachside restaurants. They had spent every waking hour since on the sun loungers lined up on the stretch of sand immediately outside his restaurant, playing a waiting game, which for Penny was the equivalent of being on death row. First of all because sitting around waiting for someone to cop off with someone else meant that you weren't supposed to talk or even think about anything else, and second, it was only a matter of time before Jackie would win him over and Penny would be expected to make herself scarce, to hop it as they said in *Carry On* films. Third, Penny couldn't help wondering that if Phoenix were still alive and if Jackie was pregnant by him, if she would still be chasing after other boys. This one had black curly hair (like Marc's!) and eyes the colour of Christmas hazelnuts. They had christened him Marco, for obvious reasons. As far as they knew it wasn't his real name. And as far as Penny could see he wasn't even working that morning.

Penny vowed that if she and her parents ever went on holiday again, never to complain when they insisted on doing something 'interesting' like visiting the house of some dead French poet that Penny had never heard of. Perhaps they would let her invite Patricia to go with them.

She looked across at Jackie in her new rainbow-striped halter-neck bikini (£2.50, Dorothy Perkins), bought especially for the holiday, and then down at the navy blue one-piece on her own body that had served her well since the second year at school despite her having grown over a foot in that time. She'd have liked to buy a new one too, but had had no money

220

for extras; as it was she'd struggled to scrape together the cost of the holiday and her ten pounds of spending money.

She picked up her book, and Jackie's sixth sense immediately honed in on Penny's attention having shifted away from her. She flipped over onto her side and sat up, with one arm crooked above her eyes for shade, while the other flicked her hair behind her shoulders.

'Is he here yet?' she said.

'Who?' asked Penny, resenting the assumption that she would stay on constant lookout for Jackie's fancy man while Jackie relaxed.

'You know, Marco.'

Dim, thought Penny. 'No idea,' she said.

'I'm thirsty,' said Jackie.

'I'm going for a swim.' Penny put her book down again and tiptoed over the hot sand towards the sea. Jackie couldn't swim, and Penny took delight in making a great show of diving, the way Phoenix had taught her, into the body of a breaking wave and emerging on the other side, sleek as an eel. But when she looked back, Jackie wasn't watching. She was wiggling her behind into the restaurant in search of refreshment, and Marco.

When Penny returned dripping to her lounger, Jackie was tapping a wooden lolly stick against a raised knee, and both of them had cooled off sufficiently to resume their friendship.

'You're getting very brown,' said Penny.

'I always do. I never burn.'

That evening, Jackie hadn't so much as looked at her dinner before she ran off to the toilets to be sick. It wasn't that bad, fish and chips, too limp and greasy when you came to eat it, but there was nothing wrong with the way they looked. Her mother declared enough was enough and got up and marched over to the holiday representative. By the time Jackie returned to the table, more olive-skinned - in the green sense - than ever, the doctor had been called, provoking Jackie to flounce off all over again, this time in fury. Penny wondered if she should follow her but Mr and Mrs Benham made light of the situation by raising their eyes skyward and insisting Penny stay and finish her dinner with them.

They continued their meal in silence. Even after Phoenix died the Jacobses' dinner table had never been that quiet, but Penny preferred silence to the Benhams asking about her parents, which they so far hadn't; it was a relief when the doctor arrived and they all traipsed up to the girls' room to see Jackie, who was lying on the bed looking quite green. The whole room stank of sick. Penny opened the balcony door for fresh air.

With the exception of a few instructions given in shaky English, the examination of Jackie's stomach was mostly conducted in silence.

'Thank you. Open.'

The doctor slipped a thermometer in Jackie's mouth. Penny hoped that whatever Jackie had, she wouldn't pass it on to her. Maybe it would be so bad that Penny would have to move into a room on her own. Fingers crossed. On the other hand, if it meant Jackie not being pregnant, Penny would happily stay and catch anything.

'Thank you. Back.'

He pushed Jackie by the shoulder until she twigged that he wanted her to lie down, and Penny hoped that if she was pregnant the baby would inherit her brother's brain. The doctor started prodding at Jackie's stomach through her new thin cotton dress (£5.95, Chelsea Girl) and Penny blushed on Jackie's behalf.

At last the doctor shook his thermometer, crossed himself and muttered something in Spanish. He beckoned to Mr and Mrs Benham to follow him out of the room. Jackie stayed lying down, hands on belly, staring up at the ceiling. Penny was wondering why the doctor had crossed himself; isn't that what happened when someone was going to die?

'What was all that about?' she asked in a loud whisper, taking care not to move closer to the bed in case she caught something.

'I'm up the spout,' said Jackie, and started giggling as if it were nothing more serious than being caught stealing sweets from her mother's handbag.

'What? said Penny. 'What do you mean?' For years afterwards, Penny would marvel at her own ability to be shocked by the revelation of something she had known all along to be true.

'Up the duff. Got a bun in the oven.'

'How do you know? The doctor didn't say that.'

Jackie's laughter became more hysterical, but Penny couldn't trust that her mirth was real; it sounded dangerously close to crying to Penny's ears, although different to her crying at the funeral. All Penny could do was stand and watch while her guilty conscience reprimanded her for not comforting her friend. Jackie hadn't thought to comfort Penny when Phoenix died; their friendship didn't stretch to sympathy.

Penny was on the verge of tears herself when the door opened again and Jackie's parents returned. Straight away Jackie's laughter crumpled into sobs and Penny realized she really had been laughing all along and that this sorrowful performance was for the benefit of her parents, who sat down on the bed on either side of their daughter. Penny watched the tears run in parallel lines down Jackie's cheeks, as if even they couldn't bear to disturb the perfect symmetry of her face. Like a Tiny Tears doll, she thought, press her tummy and she produces real baby tears.

Penny didn't know where else to look so she looked down at her lap, wondering if she should leave. But then she realized her presence had been forgotten; she would only draw attention to herself if she were to get up and walk out, and besides, all the questions Jackie's parents were asking were the same ones Penny wanted to know the answers to. And even though Jackie wasn't answering, they continued to reel them off: how long had Jackie known she was pregnant? Why hadn't she said anything? Who was the father? (Penny had a horrible feeling she already knew the answer to that one.) Had she been raped? (Yes, had she?) Why hadn't she asked to go on the pill? How did she expect them to be able to continue the holiday? What if it was too late for her to have an abortion?

Hang on a minute, Penny wanted to say, that might be my little niece or nephew you're talking about, my parents' grandchild, but she didn't want to complicate matters further, inspire yet more questions that might turn the spotlight in her direction or lead anyone to hold her somehow responsible for her dead brother's misdemeanours.

There was none of the cooing and hair-stroking that she would have expected from Jackie's accepting, forgiving, modern parents. 'Who were you expecting would raise this child?' Jackie's mother said before bursting into tears and continuing to bewail her misfortune as she blubbed: 'You're so selfish. We're too young to be grandparents.'

Oh my giddy aunt. Penny turned away to look out at the stars, trying to locate her brother among them. Not a bad parting shot for a moron, she thought, and concentrated on telegraphing that thought up into the dark blue, into the space beyond it, to wherever her brother might be concealing himself. Make me an aunty at fifteen. Smart one, our Peeniss.

She dared not even consider how this news might affect her own lunatic parents if they found out, which they never would if she had anything to do with it. But what if it was too late for an abortion and Jackie turned up with her baby at one of Katherine's Gingerbread sessions?

When she turned back, Jackie's parents had gone and Jackie was sitting up, her back resting against the wooden headboard. Her eyes were red as if she really had been crying and Penny was sorry for suspecting her of acting.

'Fuckinell our Jack, what are you going to do?'

'I'm having an abortion. I already booked it for when I get back. Becky Amblin told me where to go, I've got the money in my savings account. I should get your parents to pay for it.'

This was the confirmation Penny had been dreading. 'I didn't know you were friends with Becky Amblin,' she said. Becky Amblin was the village scrubber. Becky Amblin had had two abortions before leaving school at sixteen, had two kids already and was barely nineteen. (Rumour had it that her own father was also the father of the two kids, but Penny acknowledged that might be stretching it.) Every day she pushed her pram from one end of the village to the other and was usually heard shouting at the oldest child before she was seen.

Jackie went on. 'If he was still alive, I probably would've kept it, but there's no point now he's snuffed it.'

Penny was unclear if these words were intended to ease or heighten her distress. 'No point?' she said. 'So what would be the point if Phoenix was still alive?'

Phoenix was still alive, or a part of him anyway, inside the belly of a thick scrubber, and Penny was going to have to watch him be killed all over again.

Jackie kept quiet (was she thinking about the question, or was she just waiting for Penny to forget she'd asked it?). Penny watched her twist her hair into a knot against her bare shoulder then let it slip loose, and in that curled action she saw the image of a foetus in a jar.

'You should be in a fucking mental home,' said Penny, making for the door.

'What, with your mum?' Jackie shouted after her. 'You're only here because my parents feel sorry for you. I didn't want you to come.'

Penny slammed the door and stood in the corridor, wondering what to do next. Jackie's parents' room was a few doors down the corridor. Penny knocked at their door. Jackie's dad opened it and held it open wide for her to walk in, but she stayed put on the threshold.

'I want to go home,' she said. 'Or I want my own room.'

'Did you know about this, Penny?' said Jackie's dad.

'Bloody hell,' said Penny, and stormed off to the lift.

Penny threw a handful of shingle into the shallow water. And another. She liked the sound it made, like a music box winding down. Behind her someone was collapsing the beach umbrellas into arrowheads and dragging the sun loungers across the sand to stack one upon the other, and that someone was Marco. Penny knew it was him but pretended not to. She got to her feet; he would recognize her by her height. The sole advantage of being a freak, people recognized you from a distance. In all likelihood he would see she was alone and ignore her.

She had been compiling a list in her head of who would care if she were to die, if she filled her pockets with stones like Virginia Woolf and walked out into the sea like Reggie Perrin, and kept walking until the water was over her head. Who would cry when her empty shell was washed up in fish-nibbled pieces along the coast? Wedgie and Benn might care if Patricia stopped popping in every day and JJ stopped coming out of the shed altogether and they realized there was no one left to feed them, but even then they could probably survive on birds and mice. Her dad seemed to have forgotten she existed and her mother had never paid her much attention to begin with. She and Patricia hadn't been friends long enough for Patricia to care too much. Even in death she would play second fiddle to Phoenix: by dying first he had stolen any thunder that might rumble in response to her own demise.

Perhaps she could pretend, and leave her clothes at the water's edge. Marco could wrap her up in a tablecloth and take her back to his house. She could get a job in a tourist shop or a bar and start a whole new life.

'Hello. You are alone?' It was him.

Penny had planned to fake a little jump of surprise if he should speak to her, but in the end her surprise was real.

'Would you like a drink?'

'I have no money,' said Penny, speaking in pidgin and flapping her arms like a pigeon.

'That is okay. What would you like? Come.' He touched the bare flesh of Penny's forearm, his teeth flashing white in the dusk.

Penny's whole body tingled. She was only an inch or two taller than him, if you discounted the fact that she'd been standing in the same place for a few minutes and her feet had sunk down into the sand. He moved, she followed. She wondered how long it would take him to ask where Jackie was.

'You want a beer? Or a martini?'

Penny had tasted Martini at Jackie's house, disgusting stuff, thick and syrupy and sickly. She chose the most sophisticated drink she could think of. 'Could I have a Bacardi and coke please? I'll pay you tomorrow.' She sat down on a stool at the bar.

'No paying, this is from me. A gift to a beautiful English woman.'

Penny's face glowed beetroot.

It must have been late because the restaurant was busy with couples and families, most of them speaking English. She resisted the urge to count them, those clean people, showered and changed, scrubbed and rosy, dressed in evening wear like catalogue models or smart weekend clothes like people in advertisements for frozen food. They clinked glasses and laughed; one couple took it in

229

turns to pour sangria into each other's mouths from above. JJ and Katherine would hate it here, she thought. A brat in a suit and tie turned and poked his tongue out at Penny when he saw her looking at him. She reckoned the couples with children were eyeing with envy the couples without, while the women of the couples without children were eyeing her, Penny, jealous of the attention she was getting from Marco.

'My name is Jordi,' he said.

'I'm Penny.'

It was so romantic, like a story in Jackie. She traced the squares on the tablecloth with a fingernail as she imagined a character in a Jackie story would do. He whisked away and just as swiftly returned.

'Bacardi and coke,' Jordi said, placing the glass on the table with a flourish. 'Would you like to eat?'

'Oh no, thanks. I've had my dinner.'

'So, you didn't eat here?' he said in mock offence, pronouncing the 'h' in 'here' in the same way he had said the first letter of his name, as if he was gathering phlegm in the back of his throat, like Phoenix used to when he pretended to gob at her. Jordi wagged a finger at her and turned away to answer a summons from the besuited brat's father.

She watched him as he worked, weaving his hips between the tables like a dancer, comparing him to the woman who ran the caff in the village: plates tipping as she carried them, fag hanging from the corner of her mouth, dropping ash on the tables as she wiped them with her stinking cloth. She wondered how much he earned and if it would be enough to support them both until she found a job and if he had ever been on strike. Jordi was kind, she decided; he was friendly to all his customers and not just because he wanted a big tip, but because he liked his job and was good at it. If she did go home she pledged to be different in her Saturday job, she would smile at people, not force herself to look miserable because Jackie had told her it was the only way to avoid getting wrinkles in her thirties. Jordi would make a good husband, like her dad, he knew how to look after people, make them happy and cared about doing it. He couldn't be much older than her brother and his friends, but how much more mature and graceful and dignified he was than any of them.

Empty glass, full glass, and away he swished again. Penny was already tipsy, but she wanted to be drunk, independently of Jackie, and she wanted to get off with someone, independently of Jackie. The fact that her target was someone Jackie fancied made the challenge all the more delicious, especially as Jackie wouldn't be getting off with anyone for a while. And she was going to be a bit short of friends. Let her hang around with Becky Amblin; now she had completed her initiation into the Scrubbers' Club they were two of a kind.

The restaurant eventually emptied of families as parents, probably desperate for a moment's peace, dragged their children back to their hotels, leaving the childless couples to their candlelight and cocktails. Then Jordi was at her side, holding out a hand to help her to her feet.

'I will take you to your hotel. Where is your friend?'

At last the question Penny had been expecting, but as it was delivered with no interest beyond the desire to know the reason Penny was alone, the answer was easy.

'She's not very well,' said Penny. 'Ill. Bleurgh.' She mimed the act of puking and Jordi laughed.

'I think she like herself very much,' he said. 'Tomorrow I no work. You come with me to swim the day?'

'Okay,' said Penny. 'Swimming the day sounds good.'

They stopped at the hotel entrance.

'I meet you here. Nine o'clock. We have beautiful day.'

Penny beamed as he squeezed her hand. She couldn't wait to tell Patricia, she would send her a postcard the next day.

Their room was in darkness and Jackie was sitting out on the balcony overlooking the road that Penny and Jordi had just walked along.

'All right?' said Penny, and got a sneer in return from her friend, her ex-friend. Penny shrugged, filled with tipsy self-righteousness. So what if Jackie had seen? She hoped she had seen. If she sat there again the next day she'd see them kissing.

***

JJ PATTED HIS CHEEKS TO STOP THEM STINGING; the skin on his face, reclaimed from under weeks of curly growth, was red and raw. The recovery hadn't been easy, with his movements restricted by the narrow confines of the outdoor loo and his vision by the tighter scope of the shaving mirror. He had given up on the battery shaver after one sorry attempt weeks before. Washing his body had been no mean feat either and one which eventually proved futile, as he had to dress again in the clothes he had been living and sleeping in for too long for them to make any kind of statement about him other than a derogatory one about his sanity.

It was too warm outside for his Arran sweater so he left it off. A light jacket would have been perfect, but until he knew for certain that Katherine was coming home he would not jinx any progress by setting foot inside the house. John Jacobs, the man who sneered at superstition.

The note he had left for Penny two days before, asking her to bring him clean clothes, was still pinned to the back door, unheeded. Scraps of paper and drawing pins had provided the raw materials of all their communication in recent weeks, but even that had petered out now as she seemed to have stopped responding to his messages.

He would have to do as he was. Even if his clothes suggested otherwise, he knew he was clean underneath. People had begun looking at him, or rather looking away from him, in the street, as if he stank of urine or threatened to attack anyone who made eye contact. It was only natural to feel insulted; other people had beards, some of them were even women, and the people in the village didn't look at them that way.

He rinsed the tiny shavings that represented the second, and final, stage of his facial reinstatement from the washbasin, and swept the snippings of his beard, which had formed a thick mat at the base of the pedestal, into the dustpan. He switched off the light and stepped out into the garden, his muscles relaxing in the warmth of the April morning, which was already teasing the pores of the Doghouse walls open, warming the shed with the aroma of pine and creosote. The garden borders twinkled with rampant forget-me-nots.

His unzipped sleeping bag was draped over the washing line to air in the lilac-scented morning, its red shimmer providing a perfect backdrop for the casual floatings of white apple blossom; and there he stood, an ungrizzled bear come out of hibernation, stiff and hungry and blinking in the sunlight. He checked his watch, there was still an hour before he needed to leave.

He opened a tin of tomato soup in the shed and emptied it into a pan. He took the Primus out into the garden, put it down on the path and set the pan on it to heat. Meanwhile, he took the secateurs and cut two sprigs of apple blossom from the lowest branches of the tree. For Katherine. He tied them together with twine and stood them amongst the pens in the jam jar on his desk.

He ate his soup straight from the pan, sitting on the back porch step, recalling the summer nights that Phoenix had camped out in the garden with his friend Rob and how he, JJ, had delivered them a traditional camper's breakfast of baked beans, bacon and fried bread, which they devoured sitting up in their sleeping bags, bleary-eyed and hung over from a disco the night before. That seemed so long ago, and yet he could still hear his son's voice croaking at him to bugger off in the waking moments before his nose had picked up the scent of breakfast.

He set off on foot, deciding to walk to the hospital so that he could leave earlier and savour for longer the experience of being on his way to see Katherine for the first time in two months. If God existed, JJ would have prayed to him that day to not let her change her mind.

In the distance, an old wartime siren wailed out its weekly test and a song came into his head, one of the singles Penny had brought home one Saturday, played incessantly for a week then never again. What was the name of it? It started with a siren. He could hear it, his feet marched to its rhythm as he hit the downhill, but he couldn't remember the words, something about not having a clue WHAT to do. That one garbled line repeated itself over and over in his head as he strode over the railway bridge. He couldn't get it, the name of the song, and nor could he stop that line from repeating itself, its camp intonation more exaggerated with each round, so that by the time he reached the hospital gates he was running, but without knowing if he was running towards Katherine, or away from the song.

He was fifteen minutes early for his appointment. He stuffed the blossom twigs, which the journey had reduced to two bare sticks in his hand, into a waste bin at the hospital bus stop.

Dr Wild apologized for keeping him waiting: very generous of him, JJ thought, given that he had called him into the office at exactly the appointed time, ten o'clock on the dot. They shook hands. No Katherine. The doctor explained that she would be joining them soon; he wanted a few minutes alone with JJ first, to make sure they were both on the same page, so to speak.

JJ sat with his hands tucked under his armpits to keep them from shaking. It occurred to him that his being there, his having been summoned to a meeting with Katherine, might not have the positive connotations he had presumed. What if he was there to be told that yes, Katherine was better and ready to be discharged, but that unfortunately she wouldn't be coming home, that her notion of him as their son's murderer had inspired such an extreme lapse of trust that she could no longer bear to consider any future with him. He imagined their meeting would be part of her therapy; an opportunity to tell him to his face, tell him that the hospital had found her and Penny alternative accommodation, that Penny was in fact installed there already and waiting for her mother and no, he couldn't be given the address, they would be moving on in any case after a short while to somewhere more

236

permanent. JJ had been stupid enough to envisage only a positive outcome to this meeting, such as the doctor was outlining now if only he could calm down and listen.

Katherine was not mad, the doctor was saying, she had met herself in a dark alley, in a depression triggered by the death of their son. She had experienced the worst of her grief, as, suspected the doctor, had JJ, and although it was by no means over, her confusion around the circumstances of that tragic event had cleared. She no longer held JJ responsible for her son's death and understood that her anger at him was to a degree a deflection of her own feelings, firstly of guilt at having given in to his request for a motor bike, but also of her own powerlessness to effect any influence over her son's fate. As a result, the worst of her anxiety had subsided. Her need for medication had substantially reduced in recent weeks and the doctor expected her to be drug-free and ready to leave the hospital soon.

He proposed that Katherine spend a day at home with JJ and Penny that coming Sunday, Easter Sunday he emphasized, as if reminding JJ to buy Easter eggs. Depending on how that went, she might then stay overnight, from lunchtime to lunchtime, one day the following week, and if that were to go well then she might stay for the whole of the next weekend. Was that schedule workable for JJ? JJ nodded, any schedule was workable for him if it meant Katherine was coming home. The doctor would have to go over it again with Katherine, but if everything worked out, she could be home in a week or so.

'As I'm sure you know,' the doctor continued, 'your daughter's visits to her mother have tailed off a little, due in part to her friendship with young Patricia Cox who lives in the staff houses, a nice girl, very bright. How do you imagine Penny might receive the news that her mother will soon be home again?'

Aside from the occasional appearance of a girl's bicycle leaning Third Policeman-style against the side wall of the house, a bicycle that he recognized as neither Penny nor Jackie's because neither would be seen dead on one, JJ had seen no evidence of nor received any information from Penny about this new friendship, but if this girl was bright it was a good thing, because quite frankly Jackie had always struck him as a bit dim. But he was digressing; the straight answer to the question was that he had no idea how Penny would react because he had not seen or spoken to his daughter for days. 'I'll, um, need to talk to her about it,' he said. And before things ran ahead of themselves he had to ask one last question. 'Does Katherine want to come home?'

Dr Wild grinned. 'I can't speak for Katherine. Let's bring her in now. Unless you have any further questions?'

JJ shook his head as the doctor rose and made for the door leaving JJ feeling like the subject of an episode of *This Is Your Life* getting up from his chair to see which long-lost family member was to make an appearance from behind the screen. He heard the doctor ask Katherine if she would like to join them but he couldn't bring himself to look as the door opened and Katherine walked in.

When he did look up, she looked different; not just different to the last time he saw her, but different to any time he had ever seen her. For a start, she had forgotten her disapproval of make-up and was wearing red lipstick and green eyeshadow, not plastered on like Penny's, but in delicate shades that made her eyes sparkle as if reflecting the sheen of the silk blouse he had bought her for Christmas. JJ dropped his arms to his sides. It was all he could do to not drop to his knees and crawl to her.

'You look great,' he said.

'You don't,' she said, settling down in the third chair.

JJ could tell from her voice that she was smiling.

'I detect the hand of Catherine,' said Dr Wild, when they were all seated. 'We have another Catherine staying at John Cary House, who was head of the make-up department at Pinewood for many years.'

JJ sat with one elbow on the arm of his chair, forearm raised and his hand set in a loose fist as though he had forgotten he'd already given up the apple blossom.

Katherine broke the spell, by turning to look him in the eye. 'I'm sorry,' she said.

'I'm sorry too.'

They sat in silence - what else was there to say? - for

what seemed like an hour until Dr Wild coughed. 'Well now,' he said. 'I am wondering if we might all meet again tomorrow afternoon, how does that sound?'

Katherine nodded and JJ smiled.

JJ watched the house for hours, like a burglar, but all was quiet. Where was Penny? There he was, justly cleared of the crime that had lost him his family and on the verge of rekindling his life, only to find himself potentially guilty of that same crime all over again. Oh irony. His stomach contracted in fear as he stepped over the threshold of the back door.

The kitchen was spotless, not a stray mug or crust of bread on the counter, everything washed up and put away, the draining board shining like a mirror. The cats' bowls had been put to soak in the sink. He checked the calendar for clues. School had finished for Easter on the previous Friday, but all subsequent days were blank.

He called up the stairs.

The living room smelled of polish and the grate had been swept. Light from the window reflected off the surface of the sideboard. The armchairs were positioned to form two points of an equilateral triangle, with the television acting as third base and the settee had been pushed into the centre of the room, with a perfect diamond of a cushion propped at each end. The house had never been so clean and ordered. Madness had claimed its third victim. 'Penny!'

The notepad next to the telephone was clear of messages. JJ tried to remember the last time she had passed a message on to him. It had been slipped under his door perhaps a week before, but the exact time or even day escaped him. He couldn't even be certain he'd read it.

Upstairs, he checked the bathroom first. Everything gleamed, clean towels were folded neatly over the towel rail, a few dregs of Vim had dried out in the sink where the final swirl of water hadn't been enough to wash them away. Everything was dry and JJ was the eighth dwarf discovering that his home had been invaded by a cleaning lady. The eighth dwarf's name was Negligent.

He opened each bedroom door in turn, saving Penny's until last. He knocked before going in.

The bed was made, its candlewick bedspread pulled smooth over the mound of pillows at its head. Penny's dressing gown dangled from the hook behind the door. It would be useless to inspect the contents of her wardrobe; if he didn't know what would be there on a normal day, how would he know if anything was missing?

The Female Eunuch was gone from the bookshelf, but that told him nothing. For all he knew she'd burned it in the grate downstairs for want of proper fuel, like a victim at the siege of Leningrad.

Ah, but her toothbrush was gone. The beaker on her washbasin was empty. If she had taken her toothbrush, her absence had been planned. Was that a good thing? It was a better thing than most of the other possibilities that were running through his mind. Perhaps she was lonely and had gone to stay with Jackie, but why not tell him she was going? Beneath all the teenage posturing, Penny was not a dramatic person, she was pragmatic and conscientious, all her school reports said so and the current state of the house bore testimony to the fact.

Suitcases were kept in his and Katherine's bedroom. Of the five they possessed, he could account for two; one was in Phoenix's room, still stuffed with his clothes, and the other had been used to deliver Katherine's belongings to the hospital. Two remained in the cupboard so one was missing: the newest smartest red one, the one Penny would be most likely to choose.

He had less than twenty-four hours to find her and bring her home. Had they arranged a visit to her grandparents this Easter? There was nothing on the calendar to indicate any plans that he might have forgotten, but that didn't mean that she hadn't gone of her own accord.

He hadn't spoken to his parents since the funeral, had wanted to wait until life had settled back down, but then Katherine had gone into hospital and there was too much he didn't want to worry them with. He would eliminate possibilities closer to home before calling them.

Down in the hall, he slid his thumbnail under the letter J in the family address book. He couldn't remember Jackie's surname, had probably never known it never having had any dealings with her parents, but was correct in his assumption that Penny would have written her friend's number under the initial of her first name. And there it was, in Penny's loopy hand: Jacqui 3625. No address. He dialled the numbers and let the phone ring at the other end for five minutes before hanging up.

He sat down on the hall floor, hoping that by some magic born of his own desperation, Jackie's parents might return home and intuit his having called.

Who was the new friend in the hospital houses the doctor had mentioned? Perhaps Penny had gone to stay there to be closer to her mother, but then didn't the doctor also say that her visits had tailed off? And why would someone pack a suitcase to go ten minutes up the road? For that matter, why pack to go fifteen minutes into the village, where Jackie lived? And why hadn't she told him what she was doing? He tried Jackie's number again, but again no one answered.

The answer was clear, she must have taken herself off to Scotland to visit her grandparents. He pulled the address book from the hall table again and found the number, then levered himself up onto his knees and dialled, hoping it wasn't too late. Old people went to bed as soon as darkness fell up there, but he had lost track of time, it was still only eight, the clocks had gone back and the evenings were stretching out toward summer, he just hadn't noticed.

His parents had no telephone of their own. Mrs Cruden,

their neighbour, kept him on the phone, subjecting him to inane pleasantries, while her husband tootled next door to fetch someone. Her tone was pitying and tentative as she quizzed him on the mundanities of life in the opposite corner of the British Isles. There was no mention of Penny, a bad sign, but maybe she was deliberately avoiding the subject of offspring entirely.

JJ prayed it would be his father who came to the phone; he would be less alert to subtextual messages, not employing them himself in ordinary communication, whereas his mother was an expert. His father would be less attuned to the note of panic underpinning his son's words.

'Hello my dear, what a lovely surprise,' said his mother. An innocuous enough opening to the untrained ear, but loaded and guilt-provoking for JJ. They had lost a grandchild and their own son had abandoned them.

'Hello Mam, how are you and Fa?'
'Oh, we're well enough. Looking forward to the spring, it's been a hard winter. Is the spring with you now?'

No mention of Penny. His mother had always cocked an eyebrow at her son's approach to parenting and for him to raise the question of Penny's whereabouts straight off would set alarm bells ringing. So he allowed the conversation follow its natural course in the hope that his mother would suddenly say: 'Anyway, that's enough of me, I expect you want to talk to Penny.' But their conversation drifted on, like the prow of a canoe slicing its way through

244

a glassy pond and would have glided on forever unless he threw an obstacle into its path.

'Mam,' he said. 'I'm sorry I can't talk for long. I've a deadline tomorrow. But just one thing: did you hear from Penny yet? Katherine and I asked her to call you over the holidays and we wanted to check if she's done it yet.'

He could sense his mother's suspicion, not only at the casual tone with which the question was asked but at his sudden concern for his daughter's relationship with her grandparents, but all she said was: 'No dear, we haven't heard from her yet, but I'm sure we will, she's a good girl. You've raised her very well, but perhaps you shouldn't expect too much of her at the moment.'

Never before had his mother had to talk him down from a position of inappropriate authoritarianism, and it was done with such kindness that he had to cough to clear his throat before speaking. 'Yes, of course, Mam,' he said. 'Thank you.'

His father would have talked about the election, marvelled at Wilson's victory and come away from the phone satisfied, but his mother, he knew, would be worrying. Just as he was himself.

He tried Jackie's number one more time. He even toyed with the idea of leaving the phone off the hook while it was still ringing and running down to the village and around the estate, straining his ears for the persistent chirrup of an unanswered trimphone, but what would that achieve?

Instead, he got into the Mini and drove up to Barrow on the off chance that Penny might be hanging around in the street with her friend. It was a long shot but a worthwhile option given that the alternative was to do nothing until the next morning, a good twelve hours away yet. But the one road that connected all the staff houses was deserted except for a couple of lads kicking a ball back and forth to each other.

He spent that night on the sofa in case Penny came home late, sleeping so deeply that his guilt increased tenfold the next morning. It seemed he was incapable of behaviour appropriate to his situation. All the nights he had spent fidgeting with worry on the camp bed in the Doghouse while Penny was safe in her bed, and then the one night she might be lying dead in a ditch somewhere, he slept as calm as a Mogadon-baby. He admonished his own lack of decorum, his lack of a sense of responsibility, but then he got going; he had until three o'clock, the time of his appointment at the hospital, to find his daughter.

There was still no reply from Jackie's house so as a last resort he reported a possible fault to the operator, but they would be unable to verify his suspicion for several hours or some similar codswallop. The girl in the shop where Penny worked didn't work at weekends and so had never even heard of Penny, and the shop manager was on her day off. The onus was on Penny's new friend to have all the answers and if that avenue proved to be a cul-de-sac, his only option would be to go to the police: the same police who had informed him of his son's death, and of his wife's admission to hospital. At that moment he vowed that if anything bad had happened to Penny, his own suicide would be the only reasonable response.

At nine thirty he called Dr Wild's office to find out the name of Penny's friend, but the secretary informed him the doctor was out and unreachable until JJ's appointment at three.

He arrived at the hospital with time to spare in the hope of nabbing a word with the doctor in private, but when the doctor came hurrying down the corridor, he had Katherine with him.

Perhaps it was because he would have expected JJ to have at least changed his clothes given the positive nature of their previous meeting that Dr Wild directed his opening question at him. 'You appear to be rather agitated this afternoon, John, is everything all right?'

He was tempted to refute the doctor's observation and try for a quiet word at the end of the session, but it occurred to him that such an opportunity might not arise and he conceded at last that the best course of action might be to confess and risk the consequences. At least Katherine was already in the hospital, and at least he would have a witness to any attack he might suffer, however deserved that attack would be. 'Well,' he said.

He couldn't bring himself to include Katherine in this conversation and directed his gaze into the space between the doctor's face and the bookshelf over his shoulder. 'There is something I need to ask you,' he said. 'I need to get in touch with the girl you said Penny had become friendly with, and, um, I wondered if you could help. If you can, I mean?'

'Is Penny all right?' Katherine said, but there was no panic in her voice.

The doctor intervened. The man had been working with fluctuating minds for so long he was psychic, JJ decided. 'I'll ask my secretary to get Patricia on the phone.' He swivelled around to the desk behind him, picked up the phone and made his request.

They sat in silence for a few moments, with Katherine's unanswered question swinging like a pendulum across the centre of their triangle, and then the phone rang.

'Hello?' said the doctor. 'Hello Patricia, I'm just passing you over to John Jacobs, Penny's father.'

'Hello Patricia,' said JJ.

'Hello Mr Jacobs,' said an anxious voice on the other end. 'Are you looking for Penny? I'm really sorry, I knew she hadn't told you where she was going and I've been meaning to come and tell you myself, but my mother's been ill and I haven't had the chance.'

'Oh,' said JJ. 'Yes.'

'She's gone to Spain for two weeks with her friend

Jackie and her parents. I don't know why she didn't tell you, I think she didn't want to bother you. She only left the day before yesterday. I've been popping in to feed the cats, are they okay?'

'Oh yes, they're fine. Thank you Patricia, that's very good of you. I'm very grateful for your help. No need to worry about the cats, I can deal with them.'

'Okay. I'm sorry I didn't let you know sooner. Please send my regards to Mrs Jacobs. She's a teacher at my school.'

'Oh, I see,' said JJ. 'Yes of course, and thank you again, you've saved my life.'

No one but JJ knew that those parting words were a simple truth, and not the dramatic overstatement they appeared to be.

'What was that about?' asked Katherine.

'Well I didn't tell you before, in case it upset you. Penny's gone on holiday to Spain with Jackie's family. Patricia offered to help me to get a few things ready for your return, but I forgot to get her number from Penny before she went.'

'You let her go to *Spain*?' said Katherine, smiling.

Welcome Home

IT WAS THE END OF JUNE AND THE WEATHER was as warm as it had been in Spain. JJ and Katherine were away, driving around America in an El Camino convertible, whatever that was, on a month-long, all expenses paid (thanks to JJ's slimy boss having forced everyone they knew to make a contribution) trip. Penny had waved them off with tears in her eyes: JJ in his embarrassing old straw holiday hat, but otherwise clean and properly dressed and he'd even had a haircut; Katherine had been wearing a flowerdy (Penny had adopted the ironic use of some of Jackie's more ridiculous pronunciations) cotton maxi-dress that looked more than a little like one of the nighties they'd bought her to wear in the hospital, and now that Penny could judge her mother by Patricia's rather than Jackie's standards, she had to concede that they looked great together and that, all things considered, she had missed her mental parents and was excited that they'd be home in a few days.

Even when she had come back from Spain saying she wanted to leave St. Bernadette's and go to the comprehensive, neither one of them had raised any objection, even the most obvious one, that she was halfway through her O-levels and had her mock exams coming up. And when she opted to start taking intensive Spanish classes and to sit the exam in one year instead of the usual two, there'd been no argument about French being better, it was positively encouraged; they had even spared her a lecture when she decided to give up her Saturday job. It was as if they'd suddenly noticed she was no longer six years old.

So, that Saturday morning at the end of June, she was sitting with her Spanish dictionary open on the kitchen table, chewing at the end of a biro, stopping occasionally to pick a splinter of plastic out of her mouth, deciphering the most recent news from Torremolinos as communicated by Jordi in his neat, loopy handwriting. So far she'd worked out that he was saving up his *propinas* to come and visit her in *Inglaterra*.

Penny and Jackie hadn't spoken since Spain. Not properly. Penny had passed her in the village a few times on her way home from school with Patricia and raised a deliberately cheery 'All right?'. Jackie, who definitely wasn't pregnant any more, had scowled back at her each time and Penny couldn't help feeling guilty that she always seemed to be on her own. But Penny's feelings on the subject of her pregnancy were still mixed; while she understood the logic of Jackie not being saddled with an unwanted baby at fifteen - she'd make a terrible mother - those few cells that had been hoovered out of her body, or some of them at least, had been a part of Phoenix; that those last few scraps of his existence had been wilfully destroyed was unforgivable when the rest of him had been killed by a freak accident. Lots of people raised kids on their own, Gingerbread was full of them, it wasn't impossible.

While JJ and Katherine were away, Patricia was staying with Penny, sleeping on a camp bed in Penny's room. As it was light outside until ten o'clock, they would cycle up to Patricia's house most evenings (with Penny riding Phoenix's old pushbike) for their dinner. If they were too tired or too lazy to cycle back afterwards, Patricia's brother would drive them in his Hillman Imp. On the days they didn't go, he would call in on them anyway because, according to Patricia's mum, he was sweet on Penny and was waiting for her to tire of Jordi being so far away. Penny liked him, but he was Patricia's brother.

On Sundays, they had been cycling round to the Nurses' Home to eat Rene's Sunday roast. Remembering her first visit, Penny went only under the proviso that she would never be forced to look at the pickled foetus again.

The day that Phoenix would have come home for the summer had come and gone, marked only by his scribbled note on the kitchen calendar. JJ and Katherine would be home for the half-anniversary of his death. Penny hadn't so much as peeped around the door of his room for weeks, she couldn't bear to see it in the state he had left it, as if he had gone down to the shops for a bar of chocolate; none of his belongings had been unpacked, and she was dreading the day they would be, should that day ever come.

Penny's thoughts were so entangled in a combination of half-understood Spanish words and half-acknowledged feelings about Phoenix that she didn't register the clatter of the letterbox.

'Here's the last one!' Patricia sing-songed from the doorway, waving a battered-looking postcard.

Penny got up to snatch it from Patricia's hand, turning it over to read the message first; all their postcards so far had been written by JJ, who'd crammed so much tiny writing onto them that there'd been hardly room for the address, but this time the message was brief and in Katherine's handwriting: *Can't wait to see you! Mum and Dad xx.* JJ had been allowed to write the word Dad himself and Penny smiled as she imagined what the winning argument must have been preceding that simple action: that he should sign it himself or Penny might assume something bad had happened.

The picture on the other side of the card was of the Wrigley building in Chicago, chosen, Penny guessed, because of some misguided conviction that she was partial to chewing gum. 'Right, come on then,' she said, giving the card back to Patricia to read, and the two of them traipsed out to the Doghouse to do the honours one last time.

Penny plucked a pencil from JJ's desk and continued the line on the enormous map of America JJ had pinned to the Doghouse wall, continuing it on from St. Louis to Chicago, completing the horseshoe of their route from New York. At the same time, Patricia pinned the postcard to the map just above the Great Lakes and together they recited out loud the names of the cities Penny expected to hear stories about for the rest of her life, or at least the whole of the summer holidays: New York, New York; Philadelphia, Pennsylvania; Washington DC, Maryland; Raleigh, North Carolina; Charleston, South Carolina; Savannah, Georgia; Atlanta, Georgia; Birmingham, Alabama; Memphis, Tennessee; St. Louis, Missouri; Chicago, Illinois. Yes, they were all places of political and literary significance, and Penny would love to see them all for herself one day, but for now not one of them had the appeal of Torremolinos, Espana.

***

WE'LL ALL HAVE ONE OF THESE THINGS instead of passports before long,' said JJ chewing on a bagel, talking and eating like a true American at his last breakfast on that continent. 'Tattooed onto our foreheads.' He was fiddling with a pack of Juicy Fruit gum, examining the small rectangle of black-and-white stripes printed onto its wrapper. 'We'll be able to buy things just by thinking about them, blink twice for yes please and the next day they'll drop through the letterbox.'

Katherine laughed at the note of despair in his voice, and the dollop of scrambled egg balanced on the corner of toast she was lifting to her mouth shook and fell off. 'You've been watching too much *Tomorrow's World*,' she said, pointing the toast at JJ's nose. 'And you do realize, don't you, that what you've just described is Penny's idea of heaven?' But JJ wasn't listening; he was busy scribbling in his notebook, making notes for his final American column, to be phoned through to the office that afternoon.

JJ had scribbled his way through every mealtime since their new British Airways aeroplane had landed at John F. Kennedy airport, but Katherine didn't mind; she had a notebook of her own to scribble in, albeit with a less clearly-defined purpose.

A sequence of columns from America had been JJ's own idea; Alan Watts's reticence had been convincing at first, but he had been too easily persuaded by JJ's enthusiastic pitch ('You'll have the opinion from the street on the impeachment hearings, as history is being made!') for either Katherine or JJ to be taken in. Katherine knew bad acting when she saw it. JJ had swung it with his: 'What other local rag has *Direct from Washington! Direct from Chicago!* in its bylines?'

Already their first week in New York seemed a distant memory, shimmering in the heat haze that had risen from the thousands of miles of tarmac they'd covered. They had spent every evening of that week in the Ninth Circle Steak House in Greenwich Village, where behind the bar a long mirror was smeared with graffiti written in soap and where, twenty years earlier, Edward Albee had spotted the words *Who's Afraid of Virginia Woolf?* and been inspired. They had sat there every evening, hoping to catch a glimpse of the man who in turn had inspired their relationship.

The messages in June 1974 were less inspirational than Albee's chance treasure, consisting mainly of the phone numbers of anonymous homosexuals hoping for a pick-up and of less than cryptic political comment: *Say bye bye Dicky! Watergate? Floodgates!*

When they had asked Fred the barman if Mr Albee was still a regular, he'd said: 'I can't say for sure you'll see him, he ain't that regular of a person' and it had been enough to encourage them.

It wasn't that they wanted to speak to him, they certainly wouldn't have done anything so crass as ask for his autograph or try to befriend him and if they'd never seen him it wouldn't have mattered; all they'd really wanted was to sit and be inspired in the place that he had been inspired. And just as well, because when they arrived one evening and had their attention directed by a subtle jerk of the neck from Fred towards a table at the back of the room, Albee's demeanour was grumpy and unapproachable. He sat drinking alone, deliberately away from other people, even those he apparently knew, ordering his drinks by making barely visible gestures to Fred behind the bar. His burgeoning alcoholic's nose was a spring bulb attached to the front of his face, his low side-parting revealed his long hair to be unwashed and greasy; JJ leaned in closer to Katherine and whispered: 'Well I never, it's Alan Watts's long-lost twin';

Katherine speculated if his chunky, downturned moustache acted as a weather vane that indicated his prevailing mood and on the possibility of it, on happier days, pointing upwards.

They had tried not to stare as Albee himself sat staring at the mirror, as if waiting for inspiration to come a second time.

'You all need more coffee?' Their waitress interrupted Katherine's thoughts, dragging her back to the Chicago diner.

JJ looked up from his notebook, raising his eyebrows and Katherine shook her head. 'No, we're finished thank you,' said JJ and pulled his wallet from the inside pocket of his jacket.

Katherine slid both notebooks into her bag and they headed out into the Chicago heat, in search of the 'L' train that would take them to Oak Park.

'Right,' said JJ. 'Hemingway and Lloyd Wright, here we come.'

***

ON THEIR LAST DAY IN NEW YORK, during their final visit to the Ninth Circle Steak House, Fred the barman had bestowed upon Katherine the honour of using his towel to wipe clean a corner of the mirror. She chose a particularly inane Nixon-related slogan to eliminate, then went and sat in the seat Albee had occupied while JJ, because he had the neatest handwriting, brandished the soap and wrote the words *After Phoenix* in its place. Maybe, on his next visit, Edward Albee would see it, and maybe he might feel inspired to write a play with that title.

ACKNOWLEDGEMENTS

Very special thanks to David James, whose knowledge of
nursing practice at Barrow Hospital was invaluable. And to
Trisha Hext, Jenny MacDonald and Carol McDonagh.

Thanks also to Philippa Brewster, Hannah Wilks,
Annette Green, Umi Sinha, Lizzie Enfield and
Christopher Shevlin for agency, editorial
and general expert advice.

And to John Davison for his brilliant cover art.

To Arts Council England for their financial support and to
Myriad Editions, and last but not least, to my all friends, real
and imagined, for all other possible forms of support,
so generously given and gratefully received.

Also by Martine McDonagh
I HAVE WAITED, AND YOU HAVE COME

Chillingly believable…Sinister, scary and utterly
compelling, it is hard to believe that this strong, confident
writing comes from a debut novelist. Read it if you dare.
Red Magazine

The most disturbing utopias are those which feel
closest to hand; and McDonagh indicates how swiftly
society reverts to tooth and claw primitivism…Fans
of post-apocalyptic parables will be well pleased.
The Guardian

This book certainly got under my skin – if you
like your books dark and more than a
little disturbing, this one is for you.
Mick Jackson
Booker prize shortlisted author of *The Widows Tale*

It paints an all too convincing picture…very atmospheric
and certainly leaves an indelible imprint on the psyche.
BBC Radio 4 *Open Book*

An exquisitely crafted debut novel set in a
post-apocalyptic landscape…I'm rationing myself
to five pages per day in order to make it last.
Guardian Unlimited

A decidedly original tale…Psychologically sophisticated, it
demands our attention. Ignore it, O Philistines, at your peril.
www.bookgroup.info

This is a troubling, beautifully composed novel, rich in its
brevity and complex in the psychological portrait it paints.
Booksquawk

A story of sexual obsession and broken trust, with the sodden (and wonderfully rendered) landscape a constant, literally atmospheric presence.
Caustic Cover Critic: Best Books of the Year

I'm still thinking about this book days after I finished reading it…a thought-provoking novel that is deceptively chilling.
The Eloquent Page

Told with passion and real skill, *I have waited, and you have come* is a disturbing but rewarding read that makes a virtue of brevity and a narrow focus.
The Bookbag

This novel manages to combine the nightmare of post environmental apocalypse with a psychological thriller…McDonagh's novel is a fine example of the spec fiction genre, the changed world she has created seems eerily real.
Gaskella

Evocative and intriguing, this novel deserves an audience.
The Argus

The novel is both poignant and terrifying. The world created here is so vivid and real, it would be hard not to be moved.
Post-Apocalyptic Book Club

Martine McDonagh has worked in the rock industry for a long time and her writing still works to this tempo, to these dynamics – physical, sensual and nerve-racking.
Jean-Daniel Beauvallet, Editor *Les Inrockuptibles*

The writing touches subconscious strata; the mystery unfolds hypnotically; the reader is drawn into a parallel universe all too frighteningly real.
Lenny Kaye (Patti Smith Group)

BY THE SAME AUTHORS

MARTINE MCDONAGH

I HAVE
WAITED,
AND
YOU HAVE
COME

'If you like your books dark and disturbing, this is for you.' Mick Jackson

Lightning Source UK Ltd.
Milton Keynes UK
UKOW03f0747110913

216979UK00004B/29/P